TRAIN TO BARCELONA

95 77, 10.

TRAIN TO BARCELONA

Jean Morrant

CHIVERS

British Library Cataloguing in Publication Data available

This Large Print edition published by BBC Audiobooks Ltd, Bath, 2007.
Published by arrangement with the Author

U.K. Hardcover ISBN 978 1 405 64038 1
U.K. Softcover ISBN 978 1 405 64039 8

Printed and bound in Great Britain by
Antony Rowe Ltd., Chippenham, Wiltshire

CHAPTER ONE

The taxi sped swiftly through the brightly lit streets of Paris until the driver brought it to a sudden halt at the station entrance. 'Gare D'Austerlitz, mam'selle,' he announced to his lone passenger as he pulled on the brake. 'I hope you are not too late.'

In the dim light of the interior, Kate glanced at her watch. Eight-fifty-five—only five minutes before the overnight train was due to depart. Quickly thrusting a note into the driver's hand, she took up her travel bag and alighted, about to cross the pavement when a car slid to a standstill beside her.

'Katherine Shaw! Well, I'll be . . .' came a man's voice from the stationary vehicle and, recognising it immediately, she froze, her heart beginning to pound. Before she could gather her wits, he had leapt from the car and taken her arm in a firmly restraining grip, causing her holdall to fall to the ground.

'Pretending you don't recognise me, are you?' he hissed, his hard, bony fingers tightening painfully. 'After all we meant to each other, I think it's time we had a little talk.'

'Let me go!' she cried, turning to face the familiar features of John Thorpe. 'We have nothing to discuss.'

1

Just as Thorpe was about to respond, there came a sudden blaring of horns and his attention was caught by an approaching gendarme who, with an expression of impatience, indicated the stationary car and the congestion of traffic behind. Thorpe's grip on her arm relaxed when, desperate to escape, she took the opportunity to wrench free of his grasp to rush blindly into the station.

Suddenly, heavy footsteps sounded close behind, causing her a fresh wave of panic, but to her relief it was only the taxi driver who smilingly thrust the fallen holdall into her hand. Blurting out her gratitude, she raced for the barrier, hoping with all her heart the train was still standing in the station.

'Barcelona?' The ticket collector gestured towards a waiting train and, as he examined her ticket, she stole a hurried glance behind to see Thorpe advancing towards the barrier.

Praying that he wasn't aware of her destination, she dashed breathlessly across the crowded platform and entered the streamlined red and silver train by the first open door. And, terrified he should catch sight of her, she grasped the handle of the nearest compartment, regardless of its class.

Once inside, she drew down the blind and closed the door, leaning against it for support. As she tried to regain her composure, the outer doors closed and she felt the train pull smoothly and almost noiselessly away, rapidly gathering speed.

Suddenly, she heard the sound of footsteps in the corridor outside, and her heart gave a sickening lurch as the door behind her began to open. Swallowing hard, she turned, expecting to meet the familiar features of John Thorpe.

'Señorita?'

Startled by the unexpected appearance of the tall, dark stranger framed in the doorway, words stuck in her throat.

'Oh! I . . I thought . . .' she stammered finally. 'I thought . . .'

'You thought?' the newcomer interrupted, his tone stern, his eyes piercingly dark. 'Exactly what did you think?'

'I . . I thought you were someone else,' she managed falteringly, unnerved by his intimidating gaze.

'Then I must hasten to inform you it is most unlikely! This compartment is reserved and I expect complete privacy. I shall call the attendant . . .'

'I'm sorry, I didn't realise, but if you will allow me to explain. I do have a ticket and . . .'

'And you arranged to meet someone in my compartment?' he put in sharply.

'No!' she cried. 'Exactly the opposite, I was trying to avoid someone.'

'So, you are running away?' he pursued solemnly.

'Oh no—you're wrong—I merely wanted to

avoid him . . .'

'Him? Your husband perhaps?' he supplied swiftly, a hint of amusement lighting his dark eyes. 'You are running away from your husband?'

'He is not my husband,' she denied on a faintly hysterical note, completely at odds with her usual calm. 'And I don't intend to trouble you with my problems.'

'But I am already troubled by your presence,' he pointed out, gesturing round the compartment in an arrogant manner. 'And if it is a serious matter, perhaps it would be wise to halt the train.'

'Oh no,' she broke in hastily. 'Really, it is not necessary. If you will just allow me to pass . . .'

Remaining firmly in position in the doorway, he gave her a searching look and decided, 'Perhaps I should call the attendant, otherwise how can I be sure you are not a criminal—a person without means attempting to . . .'

'No, please don't,' she pleaded, quickly opening her bag. 'Look, I have a ticket, and my passport . . .' She broke off, choked by tears of desperation as she sought to convince him, fearing that at any moment John Thorpe may appear in the corridor behind him.

Surveying her anxious expression, the man suddenly smiled, his even white teeth brilliant against the tan of his skin. 'If I may be allowed in to my compartment,' he began more pleasantly, 'perhaps we can continue this conversation in greater comfort.'

'Of course,' she agreed quickly and stood aside for him to enter, 'though there is really nothing to converse about. Quite simply, I'll go and find another compartment.'

'Yet, by your expression, I am convinced you would prefer me to allow you to stay here—even without an explanation?' he said as he closed the door behind him and slipped the latch. And crossing to draw down the window blind opposite he asked, 'Feel safe now?' before continuing on a faint note of sarcasm, 'If you will take my advice, I suggest you choose your friends with a little more care in future and save yourself all this distress.'

'He is not a friend,' she retorted, her colour rising, 'and I don't need advice on choosing my friends, thank you.'

'But you chose to hide from this one in my compartment,' he reminded her sharply. 'Now, let us dispense with all this foolishness. I observe you are not in a hurry to leave and risk a confrontation with this man, so please be seated and stop behaving like a frightened schoolgirl.'

Smarting a little under his stern gaze, she gave him a smile of apology and sank down on the luxuriously upholstered seat. 'I'm sorry, I know I'm behaving rather stupidly, and I realise I am a stranger to you . . .'

5

'Until this moment,' he reminded her, and cupping her chin in his warm hand brought her up to face him to continue more sympathetically, 'Please, relax. You appear extremely agitated and I don't wish to add to your distress. I am not in the habit of making the acquaintance of terrified young ladies each time I take a train. In fact, I usually travel alone, but in your case I will make an exception.'

As he settled into the seat opposite she let out a wavering breath, her mind in turmoil as she strove to decide on the best course to take. She hated to impose on the dark stranger opposite, yet wondered, if Thorpe had taken this train, was he already enclosed in his compartment for the night.

Her troubled glance met that of the man opposite when, to her dismay, at the warmth of his quick smile, she felt tears come to her eyes. To hide her emotion she cast her eyes to the floor, her hair falling forward like a curtain of pale gold as she appealed softly, 'I'd be most grateful if you will allow me to remain a while longer.' But she was too late to conceal the tear which escaped to run down her cheek.

'Madre de Dios!' he exclaimed, raising his hands in a despairing gesture. 'Those blue eyes, the tears, I am helpless! I should return you to the corridor immediately.' He paused a moment, eyeing her thoughtfully before he

6

enquired, 'Tell me, do you wish to remain in this compartment until morning?'

She looked up quickly to stammer, 'It—it is very kind of you—but I didn't intend to impose on you for the whole journey. I only needed time for everyone to settle down before I ask the steward for a cabin.'

'If you have not already made a reservation I'm afraid you are going to be unlucky. I just managed to secure the last one but, as it is a double, that bunk is vacant. I couldn't book a single so it is already paid for. Let me take your bag, the steward will attend to the bunks later, meanwhile, I suggest you take dinner with me.'

'Oh no, I can't possible accept. I am already indebted to you and don't know how to repay your kindness.'

About to raise her holdall to the rack he paused, slowly returning it to the floor as he moved towards her and drew her to her feet. 'You wish to express your gratitude, little English beauty?' he said softly in deeply accented tones. 'Come closer, I will show you how.'

Before Kate could gather her wits to protest, one tanned hand moved quickly to cradle the back of her head, his other drawing her closer as his warm lips came down to imprison hers in a firm, lingering kiss.

'How dare you!' she cried breathlessly, her cheeks aflame with anger as she struggled to

7

free herself from his embrace. 'Let me go this minute! I'd rather . . .'

She broke off as he held her at arms length, his expression one of barely concealed amusement. 'Don't be alarmed,' he said gently. 'I was only testing you to help me decide if you are merely an opportunist.'

'A what?' she gasped, struggling in vain as he continued to hold her.

'An opportunist—out for the ride, as you say—a good time girl.'

'You insulting beast!' she hissed. 'My God, you've got a nerve—and a king-sized ego! Do you imagine you are so irresistible to women they will do just anything to spend a night in your compartment, travel free? You monster!'

The continuation of her contempt was drowned by his peal of laughter, and drawing her away from the door, he said, 'Come back, little one, I will not harm you,' and went on to explain, 'I had to test your reason for being here and it was the only idea to spring to my mind. If I have frightened you, I apologise, but you must admit your intrusion into my compartment was rather strange.'

Looking into his smiling face, she uttered a wavering sigh. 'I suppose I must,' she admitted, 'but I didn't expect to be put to such a stringent test.'

He shrugged. 'Perhaps you are right,' he conceded, indicating she should return to her seat. 'I have brandy in my briefcase, maybe it

8

will help you relax whilst you tell me what all this is about.'

A trifle warily, Kate stayed on the edge of her seat, smoothing down the skirt of her tailored suit whilst he unscrewed the cap from a small silver flask and filled it with the amber liquid. She took a sip and shuddered, but soon found its fiery smoothness soothing to her frayed nerves.

'You are cold, yes?' he asked, noticing the tremble of her slim body. 'I'll call the steward—he will bring blankets.'

'No thank you, I'd rather just sit here,' she assured him quickly, her colour rising under his close scrutiny.

'Not for the duration of the night, surely?'

'Yes, if you don't object, I'd prefer it. I'm very grateful to you for allowing me to stay, even for a short time.'

He shot her a faintly mocking smile. 'Perhaps we should forget the gratitude, and there is absolutely no need for you to sit there all night—I promise not to molest you in your bunk. Relax, I shall sleep soundly.'

She was about to offer a polite refusal when there came a tap on the door and he rose to admit the steward carrying a suitcase.

'Ah, you have found my luggage!' he exclaimed in perfect French and instructed the man to place it on the rack before requesting the menu. 'My friend and I will be retiring immediately after dinner,' he

9

continued, offering a generous tip. 'And we don't wish to be disturbed until we reach the border.'

Before Kate had a chance to object, the steward inclined his head and pocketed the note, and shot the stranger a knowing smile as he retreated in to the corridor.

'I do speak French so I am quite aware of what you said to him!' she confronted the dark man crossly. 'You had no right to include me in your arrangements. I shall find another compartment immediately.'

Rising to place a restraining hand on her arm, he said, 'But you must eat. I saw you rush from the taxi—you can't possibly have had time for a proper meal.'

'Thank you, but I'm not very hungry so please allow me to leave.'

'And what of the man who drove you to seek shelter in this compartment?'

'It is a risk I must take. The situation appears to have reversed—you are the opportunist—I saw the look you gave the steward . . .'

He raised a silencing hand. 'Ah, no, you saw the look he gave me. An entirely different matter, you must agree?'

'Yes, but . . .' she hesitated, biting her lip.

'Then please be seated,' he directed firmly. 'And if I frighten you in any way—though I hasten to add I shall not—you can pull the alarm and have me arrested.'

Glancing up at the alarm system he indicated she let out a sigh of resignation and sank back to her seat.

The gleam of amusement in his dark eyes faded and he leaned forward to say gently, 'That's better. Now tell me, what is your name?'

'Katherine—Katherine Shaw,' she replied, 'though, usually, I'm just Kate.'

'Katherine,' he repeated slowly in his attractively accented English. 'And I am Luis Miguel Gamez de Vendrell.'

'Then you are not French?'

'No, Spanish—well, half Spanish. My mother was English.'

She smiled. 'I remember now, you called me señorita.'

'That is better, now you are smiling and you have a very pretty smile, Kate—no, I prefer Katherine.'

'Thank you, Mister, er . . .'

'Luis,' he supplied. 'And now we have introduced ourselves, Katherine, can you tell me what troubles you?'

'I'd rather not,' she declined, suddenly tense. 'Anyway, it is far too complicated to explain.'

'I think you mean it does not concern me and I will not pursue the matter if it distresses you,' he agreed kindly. 'Instead, perhaps you will tell me where you are going?'

'Barcelona,' she told him, warming to his

11

pleasant manner. 'Do you know it?'

'I should, I live there. Yes, Barcelona is a wonderful city!' he exclaimed proudly. 'I know it well.'

'This is my first visit, though my uncle spends much of his time here. He is in business, you see, and frequently travels to Spain.'

'Ah, so you are here to join your uncle. How long do you intend to stay?'

'I'm not quite sure. You see . . .' A tap on the door interrupted her. The steward entered bearing a tray laden with an assortment of covered dishes which he placed on the small tables he unfolded from the carriage wall. He then brought in an ice bucket containing a bottle of wine.

'You must allow me to pay my share,' Kate insisted once they were alone, 'otherwise I can't possibly accept all this.'

'Certainly not—I would be insulted!' he exclaimed in mock reproach. 'I don't usually have the company of such an attractive companion on these journeys, and I enjoy a little conversation at such times.'

'And yet, at first you gave me to understand you preferred privacy,' she countered with a smile as she reached for her bag.

'Please, close your bag,' he directed firmly. 'It will be my pleasure.'

'But I hardly know you,' she protested.

He gave a low chuckle. 'How very English!

12

Do not worry, I shall deliver you safely into your uncle's keeping. Now, shall we make a start on the paté? It looks delicious, and washed down with a glass of good quality wine it should stave off any hunger pangs we may suffer before the journey is ended.'

It was more than an hour later when she allowed him to persuade her to climb into the spare bunk and rest. Immediately the steward had made up the beds, Luis had crossed the compartment to latch the door, removed the jacket of his immaculate suit and taken off his tie before he swung himself lightly on to his own bunk.

And, although they had shared an extremely pleasant conversation over the meal, she still felt apprehensive about spending the whole night enclosed in his compartment. Obviously she would have to fight the longing to drift off to sleep, but at least it was more comfortable resting this way than sitting upright throughout the long night, however luxurious the train.

She responded to his soft 'Good-night' and, from the corner of her eye, saw him turn on to his side. She had taken off the jacket of her plain light suit and now lay under the sheet still dressed in her skirt and a sleeveless cotton blouse, preferring to risk the creases rather than take it off; much, she suspected, to his amusement.

Luis was sleeping soundly now and it

crossed her mind this could be the perfect opportunity to make her escape. But did she want to leave the safe custody of this dark Spaniard's compartment? Unless she could be sure that John was safely tucked away in a cabin, to walk along the corridor would be asking for trouble. Moving restlessly on her bunk she tried to blot John's face from her mind but his image continued to torment her into the early hours. To think that she'd trusted John completely until only two weeks ago when her whole world had seemed to topple and crash. With a shuddering sigh she recalled the day when she had caught him red-handed in her uncle's London warehouse, relabelling bottles of a cheap wine with those of a superior quality. The man who had asked her to be his wife was a cheat! And not only that, he also was risking her uncle's reputation in the wine trade. John had used her to gain promotion in the business, and as her fiancé, and a partner in the firm, he would be free to come and go as he wished. True, she hadn't accepted his proposal, but the manner in which she'd had to refuse his offer was one she hadn't anticipated.

She could still picture John's face, contorted with fury, on their last meeting. 'I'll make you pay for this, make no mistake!' he'd declared savagely after he had read the telegram her uncle had sent, demanding he leave the firm immediately. And since then

14

she'd not set eyes on him . . . until this evening.

Kate was awakened by a faint buzzing sound and opened her eyes to see Luis put a finger to his wrist-watch to silence the small alarm. With a start she raised her head, suddenly aware of her surroundings and the fact she had allowed herself to drift off to sleep.

'Good-morning,' he greeted her brightly. 'No need to get up, it's not yet six o'clock. Coffee won't be here for another half hour so you can sleep a while longer if you wish.'

Although Luis had turned onto his back, she saw his lids were closed again and he appeared completely relaxed, his strong profile, with its slightly hooked nose, clearly visible against the dark background of the compartment wall. Even in repose he had the appearance of someone confident and self assured and, except for the dark shadow around his jaw and the lock of thick dark hair which had fallen onto his brow, he looked ready to face the day without giving too much attention to his grooming, whereas she felt decidedly ruffled and untidy. Perhaps if she went quietly to the wash basin mirror and attended to her hair and make-up; she could do it without being observed.

Just when she'd managed to lower her feet silently to the floor, she glanced warily across to find his eyes already upon her, glinting in

15

the dim light as he raised himself onto one elbow. Ignoring him, she took a brush from her toilet bag and smoothed down her hair before splashing her face under the tap. She noticed the cold water had brought a little colour to her cheeks . . . or was it his stare? There was something most disconcerting about having a man watch her do these simple daily tasks—especially before six in the morning!

'Not every woman can manage to look so beautiful at such an early hour,' he remarked, sliding off his bunk to land beside her.

'Sounds like you've made a study of it!' she returned a trifle tartly, aware of his closeness which she found to be curiously disturbing.

He shrugged. 'Obviously you're not used to compliments at this time of day.'

'I should think not! In fact, this is the first time in my life I've had a man watch me wash my face in the morning.'

'Or spent the night with a man in your room, by the sound of it,' he mocked. 'But there's no need to be so prickly. After all, I did keep my word.'

'Yes, I'm sorry, thank you. And now I'll move out of your way.'

Without further comment, Luis drew an electric razor from his travel bag and, plugging it into the wall socket over the basin, proceeded to shave. Kate found her eyes following the razor around the contours of his

16

strong jaw, its smooth continuous movement drawing her gaze to his sensuous lips.

With a start, she saw him studying her through the mirror, his eyes narrowed and faintly mocking as though he read her thoughts.

'I could have gone into the corridor,' she offered, her cheeks colouring slightly as he continued to regard her. 'I didn't mean to stare.'

'I rather think you enjoyed watching me,' he accused with a devilish grin. 'And in case you've never seen a man change his shirt before, you'd better close your eyes.'

'Don't be ridiculous!' she snapped. 'I've seen hundreds of men on the beach, so what's the difference?'

'Ah, very different,' he disagreed, starting to undo the buttons of his shirt. 'In this enclosed space—and alone with me—ha, you're actually blushing!'

Kate rose quickly to her feet and turned her back on him. 'You may be used to this kind of thing,' she accused crossly, 'I'm not! But, as it's your compartment . . .'

She heard his throaty chuckle and the rustle of fabric and, after a few moments when all was quiet, turned back to see him tucking a fresh silk shirt into his slim fitting trousers. His shirt was still open to the waist, and in that one hurried glance, before she hastily averted her eyes, she caught sight of his

17

muscular chest and its covering of fine dark hair.

Furious that he should find her embarrassment amusing, she gave an exasperated sigh.

'Don't tell me you have never seen a man's chest before? How old are you—twenty one?'

'Twenty-four, actually, though I don't see what my age has got to do with it!' she retorted hotly.

'You're a funny girl,' he said gently, turning her round to face him. 'I thought the English had now lost a great deal of their reserve, but it appears I was wrong. Perhaps a cup of coffee will help make things seem more normal—I'll buzz the steward.'

In minutes the steward was there with a tray. 'Sleep well, sir?' he asked Luis, in French, setting it down beside them.

'Extremely,' Luis replied, adding strong emphasis to the word and, with a sigh of feigned dejection, ended in soft English, 'I'm sorry to say,' as the steward was leaving.

'You're determined to embarrass me!' Kate flared after the door closed.

'Don't you enjoy a little teasing?' he asked. 'Where's your British sense of humour? It is supposed to be one of your strong points.'

'Teasing, yes, but . . .'

'But what?' he interrupted, his eyes sparkling as he leaned closer. 'Could it be you are a trifle piqued because I kept my word?

18

Would you rather I had swept you into my arms? We Spaniards are very passionate lovers.'

'I'm not interested in your reputation!' she retorted angrily. 'I'm grateful for your hospitality, but that's as far as it goes and, before we part company, I intend you shall take payment for half the cost of this compartment, also my dinner.'

'Not now,' he said impatiently and, gesturing towards the coffee pot, directed, 'Perhaps you will pour whilst I attend to my notes for the day.'

Without a word, she proceeded to pour the coffee, and as she drank she looked on while he opened his diary and ran a well manicured finger down the page. Making his notes, he appeared composed and businesslike—so different from the jovial, teasing traveller of only moments ago.

Glancing up, she found him gazing thoughtfully into space as he sipped his coffee until as if sensing her eyes upon him, he returned his attention to her and smiled.

'Very soon we shall reach the border,' he said pleasantly, 'when they change the gauge of the wheels to suit the Spanish track, but it doesn't take long; we're due in Barcelona at eight-thirty or so.'

'It's a very efficient means of travel,' she agreed. 'Sometimes my uncle doesn't arrive until mid-day if he takes the other train.'

'Is your uncle meeting you at the station?'

'Yes, at Paseo de Gracia, by the information office. Where will you leave the train? I believe there are at least three main stations.'

'Quite correct, but I shall be leaving the train with you.'

'If you're going to the same station,' she said, 'I shall know where to get off, just in case I miss the sign.'

'I shall leave the train with you to ensure you don't get lost. There's more than one exit, and I'd like to deliver you safely into your uncle's keeping.'

'Oh, Luis, how old fashioned that sounds. I'm not a child you know!'

'But what of the man you've been hoping to avoid? He may be heading for the same place.'

Her smile faded. 'I never thought of that,' she confessed meekly. 'In fact, you've made me forget all about him.'

'Bueno! That is what I hoped, and there's still time to tell me about it, if you wish?'

For reasons unknown to her, and quite foreign to her nature, Kate found herself confiding in the man opposite—a complete stranger, until the previous evening—telling him why she chose to hide in his compartment, and the events which led up to her journey. He listened with interest, giving the occasional nod of encouragement until she had concluded her story when she sat

20

back, giving him an apologetic smile.

'I'm sorry, I've just realised I have been talking about myself all this time. You must be bored.'

'Quite the opposite—it's a fascinating story. Your uncle was right in dismissing him, and you were brave to not let him have the list of new outlets for dispatching wine even if he had acquired the contracts himself. And now I can appreciate why you acted as you did though, surely, he can do you no real harm? Have you tried threatening him with the police? That should put an end to it for good, and he's not going to get very far in Europe without the sound backing of a reputable firm—that is, assuming he's on a business trip.'

'I didn't want to involve the police, though if you'd seen the expression on his face when he demanded I hand over the contracts, it was frightening,' she told him, her expression growing anxious. 'I'm not willing to risk finding out exactly what he meant by his threat.'

'Of course, I am sure you are right. At least you will be safe with your uncle. And yet, I wonder why Thorpe also chose to come to Spain—could it be he's buying again?'

'I wondered that too, but he's sure to have made friends here, so I expect he's simply visiting.'

'Friends!' Luis laughed. 'More likely they'll

21

be rogues. Strange you should choose to associate with such a man though, I suppose, having to keep the business going after the death of your parents gave you little chance of a full social life. Did you have many boy friends?'

'No,' she admitted, 'they soon tired of me. I couldn't get out a lot and John seemed to monopolise most of my free time during the two years since my parents died when I had to help my uncle in the business.' And, with a rueful little smile, she added, 'What a fool I was to think he cared for me when really he was only furthering his own position in the firm and, to make matters worse I was the one to persuade my uncle to promote him.'

'Were you heartbroken?' Luis asked. with kindly concern. 'After all, it must have come as quite a shock to learn he was a traitor to the business?'

'A shock, yes, but heartbroken . . .?' She paused a moment before continuing with, 'Strangely enough, no. It all happened for the best, I realise that now.'

'But you lost a lover,' he persisted. 'Surely you miss him?'

'A lover!' she cried indignantly. 'He was not my lover, and I consider that to be a nasty presumption on your part. In fact, I've never . . .' She halted, her colour rising in confusion.

'You have never had a lover, I think you were about to say?' he interjected with a quirk of his lips. 'I'm surprised as I was given to understand most English girls have relaxed their principles these days—is that not so?'

'I'm not most English girls!' she snapped. 'Also, my morals are no concern of yours! I must have been mad to divulge my private affairs to you, and now I suppose you'll have a good laugh at my expense!'

'Of course not,' he responded crossly. 'And, while you're with me, your morals are my concern, otherwise why do you think I allowed you to remain in my compartment? I would never have forgiven myself if you had got into some kind of trouble on this train.'

She gave an apologetic little shrug and wondered how it was that he always managed to change everything round to his advantage. At times he could be almost aggressive in his accusations, then quite suddenly he would become the sympathetic listener, his voice gentle and consoling. Was it possible his concern was genuine, or was he merely playing games with her emotions?

'Hey, Miss Daydream! I said we are approaching Gerona so it is not far to Barcelona now.'

'Oh, I'm sorry, I was miles away.'

'Were you wondering how to account for my presence when you meet your uncle? I don't intend leaving you until he arrives. Incidentally, where will you be staying?'

'I won't know until we meet. It could be a

23

hotel, but I expect it will be with friends.'

'Pity, I was hoping to contact you again whilst you're here. I could show you the city and take you to dinner in one of the many famous restaurants. Would you like that?'

'It's most kind of you, but I rather think my uncle will want me to travel with him on business,' she explained, 'and we've got to discover where those labels came from as soon as possible.'

'Then I shall request your uncle's permission that he spare me a little of your time,' he said decisively. 'I am quite sure he will be willing to allow you some freedom.'

'Allow me!' she gasped, dissolving into fits of laughter. 'Really, I've never heard anything so old-fashioned.'

Luis compressed his lips, his eyes darkening. 'Your behaviour is most unbecoming,' he reproved, 'and I was being quite serious.'

'Then perhaps we had better get something straight,' she snapped, recovering quickly. 'I can go wherever I please without having first to gain my uncle's permission. And, that being so, you'll ask him no such thing!'

'He may be only too relieved to know you're in good hands,' he countered with an air of arrogance, his dark head erect as he surveyed her from the seat opposite. 'Up to now you haven't proved you can do very well on your own.'

With rising anger, her blue eyes flashing, Kate retaliated. 'You've got a nerve!' she cried furiously. 'I suppose you think that sharing your compartment with me gives you the right to dictate what I must do? Merely to boost your own ego, you consider me as a damsel in distress and find it highly amusing. Well I'm not the kind to be fooled by your charms, señor, and I may be considered a second class citizen in your country, but I refuse to be thought of as a plaything just because it amuses you!'

For a moment his eyes seemed to grow even darker, and she saw a flash of anger cross his face, which he managed to suppress before giving one of those typical Latin shrugs, followed by a mirthless smile, and said carelessly, 'A plaything? Yes, I had considered you in that position. But a second class citizen, never! You should get your facts straight, young lady, we Spaniards are more modern minded than you realise, particularly in Barcelona.'

'You surprise me!' she retorted. 'I thought women here were shackled to the kitchen sink with half a dozen children clinging to their skirts.'

'So you don't like children and the domesticity entailed in their upbringing?'

'I didn't say that,' she snapped. 'You're twisting my words again.'

'But you don't consider a loving husband

25

sufficient compensation for the chores of family life?' he suggested enquiringly. 'Yet some women are quite content with such a life, are they not?'

'Well, I wouldn't care to be treated as a slave.'

He gave a throaty laugh. 'A masterful husband may be just the thing you need if you're going to continue flying off the handle each time you wish to voice an opinion. If your uncle hasn't managed to tame you before now, perhaps a good man could!'

CHAPTER TWO

It seemed to Kate that mile upon mile had passed before the train finally drew into the station. Once in the city, the track had run along behind tall buildings; some of them shabby with lines of washing at every window, bright flowers cascading from their window-boxes.

'Almost there,' Luis told her, reaching down for her holdall. And, gathering together his own luggage and briefcase, took a quick glance around. 'I think we've got everything, and at least you have arrived in Barcelona safely.'

Kate smiled, her heart beginning to pound in anticipation, but when Luis made to slide back the door, the sound of footsteps in the corridor caused her to hang back in case John was waiting to alight.

'Will your uncle come on to the platform or wait for you outside?' Luis asked, hailing a porter through the open doorway. The man immediately hurried forward.

'I'm not sure . . .' she faltered, suddenly grateful for his concern. Arrogant and self-assured though he may be, she knew he would see to it that she came to no harm and, in a country so new to her, she may have to rely on his help.

'Well, if he's not on the platform I could install you in the bar whilst I go outside and search for him.'

'Oh no,' she begged, clutching his arm. 'Please don't leave me . . .'

'Don't worry, I won't,' he assured her quickly, giving her hand a comforting squeeze. 'I've grown quite fond of you during these past twelve hours—tantrums included!'

With the luggage now in the hands of a porter, he led her towards the exit and, alighting from the train, reached up to take her hand, even though the step down from this particular train was nowhere near as steep as was usual on continental railways. The porter soon had their baggage on a trolley, leaving them free to stroll along the platform, and she had just paused to check her bag was closed as Luis continued ahead when, suddenly, she sensed someone close behind and, turning, saw John regarding her, his expression one of unconcealed triumph.

'Thought you were on this train,' he said, reaching out towards her. 'Now, perhaps we can continue where we left off, and this time without interruption!'

Kate shrank back from his outstretched hand, her heart lurching uncomfortably. And she had just managed to utter a cry of protest when Luis stepped between them.

'Please refrain from pestering my fiancée!' Luis snapped, his tone menacing. 'Otherwise,

28

I shall have no alternative but to call the police!'

'Your what?' Thorpe demanded sharply, his mouth tightening to a thin line as he glanced across at Kate. 'Did he say . . . ?'

'You heard me, man!' Luis broke in, his voice clipped but low. 'Now leave us!'

Kate saw John's mouth open as though he was about to further his protest, but obviously thought the better of it and, throwing her a hard glance, he turned and stalked off down the platform.

She heard Luis take a deep breath as though to shake off his anger before he looked down at her and smiled. 'That should be the last we see of him!' he said, but Kate wasn't so sure. John seemed bent on taking his revenge, and there was still the matter of the papers she carried. She clutched her bag more tightly to her and shuddered, even though the atmosphere in the station was heavy and warm. Perhaps John didn't realise she was carrying the new contracts with her; even so, the sooner they were safely in her uncle's hands, the better.

'I'm very grateful to you,' she began, trying hard to stifle the quiver in her voice as his hand rested on her shoulder. 'I don't know what I should have done if you hadn't been here.'

'Given in to his demands, I expect. I must say, your friend is a mean looking character.'

29

'He's not my friend!' she cried brokenly. 'Oh, I do wish Uncle Clive was here as I don't suppose John believed you, even though you managed to send him away. I just wish John would just leave me alone!'

'If what you have told me is true, he deserves far more than that! Don't worry, I'll stay with you until your uncle arrives, just in case he guessed I was merely protecting you. Yet, come to think of it, it might not be such a bad idea, perhaps it's time I took a wife.'

'Perhaps it is!' Kate laughed, her blue eyes shining as she cast him a flirtatious glance and, now more relaxed, continued, 'Seriously though, I can't keep on thanking you, but I intend my uncle shall learn of the help you have given me. I know he will appreciate it . . .' She broke off suddenly as Luis attracted her attention when there came an announcement over the station speakers. At first she couldn't understand a word that was spoken until the speaker's voice changed to heavily accented English after she heard her own name. 'Señorita Katherine Shaw,' the voice repeated, 'Please go to Hotel Estrella with taxi.' The announcement was repeated once more, then silence when she turned to Luis enquiringly, her expression becoming more anxious.

'Do you suppose the message is genuine?' she asked. 'I mean, could John have . . . ?'

Luis shook his head. 'I know what you are

thinking, but no, he has not had the time; I'll tell you what, just in case there is something wrong, I'll go to the hotel with you and make sure it is not a hoax. I'd feel much happier knowing you were safely in the hands of a relative before I leave. You may not have realised, Thorpe could have heard the announcement, too.'

'You could be right, but I seem to be putting you to an awful lot of trouble.' She sighed, glancing up to meet his look of concern to add, 'I'm lucky to have met you.'

'Exactly!' he interposed. 'And to repay your debt you will allow me to take you to dinner tonight. It sounds as if your uncle is staying in the city for today, at least.'

Giving him a quick smile, she nodded. 'I'd like that, thank you, though, I must discuss it with Uncle Clive first.'

'Naturally, and should he have made a previous arrangement for this evening, then I shall expect to see you tomorrow, instead. Now, let us find a taxi, you must be feeling exhausted after such a stressful journey.'

Kate found the taxi ride through the city to be quite alarming. The car seemed to tear along the busy streets at such a speed she couldn't fully appreciate the numerous places of interest Luis pointed out to her as they travelled.

With a screech of brakes, the vehicle finally pulled up in front of the hotel when Luis

31

insisted upon paying the driver, dismissing him, deciding he could command another when he had satisfied himself that everything was in order.

At the reception desk Luis spoke to the receptionist, a polite bespectacled young man, who immediately reached for a slip of paper bearing a telephone message for Kate .

'I'll translate for you,' Luis offered, leading her to a nearby settee. 'It is from a Señor Clive Shaw . . . your uncle?'

'Yes. Is something wrong—why isn't he here?'

'No, and if you will just be patient for one moment I will tell you why,' Luis said and, returning his attention to the note, continued, 'He apologises for not being at the station but says you are to stay here tonight and he will join you tomorrow evening . . .'

'But where is he now?' Kate interrupted again and then with a gasp of alarm asked. 'You do think this is genuine?'

'Yes I do' he replied patiently, 'but in case there is the slightest doubt, I have a suggestion to make after you have heard the rest. It appears there is a strike at the airport, that being the reason for his delay. And, as he is in the south, to take a train will entail a much lengthier journey, so that is why he will not be here until tomorrow. You do understand?' he ended, handing her the note. 'It's unfortunate but at least you know

32

he is all right.'

With a sigh of disappointment, Kate tucked the slip of paper into her bag. 'Yes,' she agreed,' I understand perfectly, and thank you again. But, before you go perhaps you will leave me your address. I know my uncle will . . .'

'Hey, not so fast!' he exclaimed. 'You haven't heard my suggestion yet. In case there is any doubt as to the authenticity of that message, I think you would be wiser to spend the night elsewhere. I have an apartment in town you could use until your uncle arrives, you would be equally comfortable there.'

Kate turned to him in surprise, amazed by his generous offer. 'Thank you, but you have done more than enough already.' she said, then quickly noting the intensity of his gaze, added dryly, 'And perhaps the authenticity of that note is not the only thing I should doubt?'

Rising to his feet, he regarded her speculatively, one brow raised. 'So, you prefer to risk a visit from Thorpe rather than accept my hospitality—yes?' he queried and before giving her the opportunity to reply, added warningly, 'I am quite sure he would hear the announcement at the station, so he knows exactly where to look for you.'

Put to her so bluntly, Kate had to agree he was most probably right. She didn't want to face John alone, here, yet the mocking gaze of the dark-eyed Spaniard infuriated her so much she gave into the urge to cut him down to size by saying, 'To me it appears to be a sort of frying pan or fire situation, don't you think?'

'Or it could be that under that cool exterior burns a longing to return to his arms?' he countered with a mirthless smile. 'Come, give me your travel bag and I shall ask the receptionist to call for a taxi. I can leave my telephone number here in case there are any further messages.'

It was less than half an hour later when Kate stepped from the taxi after it had pulled up outside an impressive old building standing beside a tree-lined road, away from the bustling city centre.

Luis directed the driver to place their luggage in the hallway and paid the fare before ushering her inside.

She had noticed a gleaming brass plate beside the huge wooden door and assumed the building to be divided into separate apartments as there were at least five bell pushes beside it. The entrance hall was a large tiled area with little light coming in through the shuttered windows on the staircase and, after the heat of the sun outside, the coolness there sent a shiver through her slim body.

As she looked around her, wondering which direction Luis intended to take, he nodded towards the door ahead, saying, 'I'm on the second floor but, thank goodness, we have a lift so we don't have to haul our luggage up the stairs.'

Standing aside whilst he opened the heavy lift door, she stared in amazement at the wrought iron lift gate within, fascinated by its intricate design. Luis drew it aside and switched on the interior light before beckoning her inside when he brought in their luggage and closed both doors.

'Rather beautiful, don't you think?' he asked, pressing one of the buttons on the polished panelling. 'It's very old and breaks down occasionally,' he added with a smile, 'but it was serviced only recently so we should make it upstairs.'

'It's fascinating,' she agreed. 'Less claustrophobic too. I'd rather be trapped in here than in one of those modern box-like things.'

'Even with me?' he queried with a twinkling gaze. 'It could be far more dangerous than any railway compartment. After all, there's no steward to come along and save your virtue here.'

'The Hotel Estrella has your number,' she reminded him, 'so someone already knows my whereabouts.'

'Can you be certain I gave them this number?' he asked drily, his eyes never leaving her face. 'You weren't there when I wrote it down.'

'Now you're trying to frighten me as well,'

35

Kate accused crossly, 'but it won't work, and I do wish you'd stop,' she ended, shrugging his hands away.

'I must say, you are a very trusting young lady,' he remarked, turning to slide back the iron gate. 'You could very easily run into trouble this way.'

'Do I take that remark as a warning?' she retorted, with a challenging lift of her chin. 'If so, then I'll go straight back down and take my chances in the hotel!'

Taking up their luggage with effortless strength, he gave a throaty laugh .

'Brave too,' he commented, as he swung ahead of her along the dimly lit landing to halt before a door at the end.

Strolling back towards the apartment door with casual grace, he took a key from his pocket and inserted it in the lock and, glancing over one shoulder as he pushed open the door, said, 'I make excellent coffee, and as you've come this far, don't you think you ought to come in and try it? If it had been my intention to molest you, I would have done so before now.'

Once inside the apartment, Kate took in the elegant beauty of her surroundings, from the graceful brocade-covered chairs to the windows, each heavily draped with exquisite lace. And, when he switched on the light, her eyes flew to the high ceiling where a crystal chandelier hung from the centre, sparkling in

36

its own light. It was a truly splendid room, furnished with good taste, and much of it, she guessed, was antique.

'You like it?' he asked, noting her interested gaze as he beckoned her to a chair. 'I find it very useful when I'm in town.'

'It's beautiful,' she agreed enthusiastically, seating herself in a comfortable arm chair, 'You have excellent taste.'

'Thank you. I've collected a few items myself, but many of the antique pieces came from my old home. It was much larger than the place we live in now.'

'We?' she queried. 'Your family, do you mean?'

'Yes, my father and my aunt,' he told her and, with a faintly meaningful look, added, 'I have no wife—in case you were wondering.'

'Oh,' she managed softly, furious because of the rising colour in her cheeks. Why did he always manage to make her feel so ill-at-ease? What did she care if he had a family or not—it was his present intention that worried her most.

Excusing himself, Luis went off to the kitchen to make coffee, leaving her to gaze thoughtfully through the lace-curtained window. John would never find her here, she was certain, and she had only the owner of this apartment to thank for that. But what of the owner? Used to leading an independent life, what was she thinking of allowing him to

37

persuade her to come here?

'That's a very thoughtful little smile,' Luis remarked as he came quietly into the room. 'What are you thinking?'

'Nothing really' Kate answered quickly, startled by his intrusion into her thoughts 'I'm just admiring the view.'

'Ah, so you have spotted the mosaic spires of Gaudi's cathedral. Remarkable, isn't it? I will take you to have a closer look in the morning as I have nothing pressing to attend to for the next day or so.'

'Oh no, I couldn't possibly . . .'

'Your uncle will not arrive in Barcelona until quite late in the day, so we will go in the morning,' he decided. 'Now, how do you like your coffee?'

'Just the way you take yours,' she replied, with feigned sweetness. 'After all, you usually know best!'

'Perhaps I ought to add sugar to yours,' he countered with an ironic smile, setting a cup and saucer on the polished walnut table beside her.

Kate compressed her lips and glanced away. 'I'm sorry,' she murmured. 'After all the trouble you have gone to, it was unkind of me.'

'No trouble,' he said, pouring the coffee from a silver pot, adding flippantly, 'I couldn't very well leave my fiancée stranded— could I?'

Kate glanced up quickly, in time to catch his enquiring look, his eyes growing darker as her lips parted to respond. But the intensity of his gaze silenced the laughing retort she was about to make and she quickly returned her cup to the tray and rose to stand by the window.

'Where is your home now? I mean, where does your father live?' she began, a trifle shakily, attempting to break the silence which had fallen between them. And when he didn't reply, continued with, 'Is it far from here?'

Rising from his chair, he came to stand beside her when, unaccountably, her heartbeats quickened at the feel of his shirt sleeve brushing her arm and the scent of his cologne as it drifted her way.

'It is approximately nine kilometres from here,' he answered finally, 'to the south of the city, away from the noise and traffic. You, and your uncle, must visit my home—I am sure you will find the foundations of your business most interesting.'

She shot him a look of interested surprise. 'You mean —you are in the wine trade, too?'

'Growing is my business,' he stated proudly, 'and naturally that increases my interest in your Mr Thorpe. It pays to keep ones eyes open for men of his kind; I have the high reputation of our good wines to consider.'

'Of course,' she agreed thoughtfully, 'and perhaps my uncle can be of help to you in that respect.'

'I look forward to meeting him. Now, how about lunch? I am sure you must be hungry and there's a nice little restaurant not far from here—that is, unless you have other plans?' he ended with a satirical smile.

'I'm quite sure you know I haven't, so I must rely entirely on your choice. But this time I must insist on paying my share.'

'Nonsense!' he responded firmly. 'You are a guest in my country, so it is my pleasure to escort you. But, should your uncle choose to invite me to dine with you both sometime in the near future, that is a different matter.'

Lunch was a relaxed and lengthy meal taken in the cool atmosphere of a small, but traditional, Catalan restaurant. Luis introduced her to the dishes of the region, suggesting she try small portions from the varied menu which he translated with casual ease. She found the platter of assorted fish to be excellent, and the accompanying wine well suited to her palate, and the delicious nougat they had to finish was washed down by strong dark coffee.

'Would you care for a liqueur?' Luis enquired when the waiter returned to their table.

'I couldn't manage another thing,' Kate declined. 'I feel quite sleepy already. Perhaps I drank too much wine.'

'I would have thought you were used to it,'

40

he smiled. 'Never mind, you can sleep it off if you wish. I have one or two matters to attend to in the city and I shall collect my car from the garage whilst I'm out, so you will be free to do as you please.'

'Otherwise?' she queried, a slight smile playing on lips as she held his gaze across the table.

'Otherwise,' he echoed, his dark eyes narrowing, 'I would expect my fiancée to entertain me—no?'

Kate chose not to reply; a tinkle of laughter escaping her parted lips as he rose to pull back her chair, his eyes never leaving her face, even when he raised a hand to catch the waiter's attention.

Outside, in the heat of the afternoon, Kate removed the jacket of her plain suit, enjoying the warmth of the sun on her bare arms, its heat penetrating the flimsy material of the sleeveless blouse she wore beneath. She sensed Luis' eyes upon her and experienced a curious tingle of pleasure as they strolled along the pavement. And when she felt his hand at her elbow to guide her across the busy street a flood of colour rushed to her cheeks.

'Nervous ?' he asked, once they reached the other side.

'Of the traffic, yes,' she agreed hastily; 'It does seem to move more quickly here, and on the wrong side which is rather confusing.'

'To us, it is the right side,' he reminded her.

41

'But I must admit we do drive a little. more recklessly at times.'

'I can understand why Uncle Clive likes coming to Barcelona,' she said, with a sigh. 'I wish he was here now.'

'Are you so disappointed?' he asked as they reached the door of his apartment. 'Never mind, tomorrow you will see if he approves of your choice of marriage partner.'

'Really!' She uttered a cry of exasperation. 'You're taking all this a bit too far. I know he'll want to thank you for all you've done for me but . . .'

'I do not want gratitude,' he interrupted firmly, 'just your uncle's permission to marry you.'

'My uncle's what?' she gasped, halting in the doorway of his apartment. 'Now look here, I don't mind a joke, but . . .'

'It is no joke, querida,' he stated calmly, ushering her inside. 'I want an English wife, and you would suit the role perfectly.'

She laughed in her amazement, and countered, 'And don't I have a say in the matter? Do you imagine I am eager to fall in with your wishes because of the shelter you offer?'

'That has nothing to do with it,' he said, gesturing round the apartment. 'My villa is in need of a mistress and you are ideal for the part.'

'How very convenient for you,' Kate

managed coolly, suppressing the fury that threatened to burst from her at any moment.

'How cool you English can be,' he returned sardonically. 'Can't you show more enthusiasm than that?'

'Enthusiasm!' she almost shrieked. 'If this is not a joke, do you think I would consider such a proposition seriously? I hardly know you, so just how enthusiastic do you expect me to be? However long I'd known any man, I would never marry him for the reasons you give. A mistress for your villa, indeed! When I choose to marry, it will be for a very different reason.'

'Would love be that reason?' he broke in, a harsh note creeping into his voice. 'Pah! A ridiculous emotion. I would have thought you had left your teenage dreams behind you long ago!'

Speechless, Kate stared at him, her blue eyes bright with anger. 'No, you are being ridiculous, señor!' she cried, finally finding her voice. 'And you're the most arrogant beast I've ever met, and I think it would be a good idea if I leave at once!'

'I should have expected such a stupid reaction from an English girl,' he gritted scornfully. 'All this sentimental rubbish.'

'Then why the devil are you so intent upon marrying one?' she snapped. 'It doesn't make sense!'

'They possess certain good qualities,' he replied with infuriating calm. 'Perhaps a lack

43

of warmth, but different—like possessing a rare painting—and beautiful, but also a challenge. A Spanish girl knows her duties; they have been tutored over the years, but a man enjoys a challenge—someone he can lick into shape.'

'Lick into shape!' Kate nearly choked on the words. 'With such antiquated ideas I'm not surprised you're still a bachelor. No-one with any sense would agree to marry you!'

'I think you would enjoy a little masterful handling, although you won't admit it. However, enough of such trivial matters for the moment—we'll see what your uncle has to say.' He smiled and reached for his jacket.

'I can tell you that now,' Kate almost screamed after him as he swung round and picked up a set of keys.

Glancing over his shoulder he shot her a devilish smile and, indicating a door across the hall, said lightly, 'Enjoy your siesta. I may be out for quite a while.

'Now just a minute,' Kate began as he retreated down the hall, but ignoring her he went out through the main door, turning his key in the lock behind him.

Kate's immediate reaction was to rush after him but when she heard his footsteps fade, the lift gate rattle, then silence, she knew it was useless. With her fists clenched in anger, she stared at the heavy door. How dare he lock her in like this! What right had he to assume she wanted to stay now that he had revealed he wished to marry her? She was so furious she couldn't think clearly and, for a full five minutes, paced up and down the hall flinging useless insults at his name. When eventually she calmed a little, she recalled his contempt for love and its accompanying emotions; how he had voiced his opinion with disdain; and as her anxiety subsided, she believed he wasn't likely to return and molest her. She was convinced he valued her uncle's approval too highly for that.

With fresh determination, she wandered back to the sala and sank into a chair, and it was not long before tiredness overcame her and she found herself nodding in her seat. Barely able to fight off the longing to drift into sleep, she remembered that Luis hadn't sounded as though he would return for some time. Her thoughts then flew to the siesta he had suggested and, unable to resist the idea for a minute longer, she went out into the hallway in search of the guest room.

There were two doors leading off one side of the hall and one, she remembered, Luis had opened to set down his cases. That one she guessed was his room so, entering the next which appeared unused, it was so immaculate, she slid off her blouse and skirt and let her sandals drop to the floor as she lay down on the wide double bed. In the semi-darkness of the shuttered room, her lids quickly drooped

45

and she was carried into deep sleep.

Kate had no idea how much time had passed when she awoke to see narrow shafts of sunlight slanting low through the slats of the shutters. She sighed in contentment until an awareness of her situation came flooding back. And it was as she stretched out her arm to glance at her watch that she realised she was not alone.

'Sleep well?' a deep masculine voice enquired, and she gasped in alarm, struggling to cover herself with the bed-spread which had been thrown back in her sleep.

But the weight of the body beside her prevented her using the cover as protection and, uttering a cry of protest, with her arms crossed over the low neckline of her slip, she started to rise from the bed.

'Be still!' Luis commanded, reaching out a strong arm to draw her back onto the pillow. 'There's no reason to rush.'

'Why didn't you tell me you were coming straight back?' she demanded angrily. 'And what are you doing in here?'

'It's almost seven o'clock,' he announced, raising himself on his elbow. 'I've been out for hours. You were fast asleep when I returned.'

'Seven o'clock?' she spluttered, fighting against his strength. 'It can't be—and why have you come into my room?'

'Your room?' he queried, with a gleam of amusement. 'I'm afraid you are mistaken, I

46

have used this room for the last six years.'

'Then why did you suggest, I rested here?' she objected furiously. 'And will you please let me go, this minute!'

But Luis maintained his grip, and however hard she twisted and squirmed, he merely laughed at her useless efforts to free herself when she became more angry than ever.

'Let me go, you beast!' she cried breathlessly. 'All that talk about not molesting me . . .'

'I'm not attempting to molest you,' he interrupted with irritating calm. 'I'm just trying to engage you in normal conversation. If you will just be quiet and listen for one moment . . .' he appealed, but Kate simply refused by continuing her fight for freedom.

'Damn you!' he hissed, and pinning her arms behind her with one powerful hand, he cupped her chin in the other and brought down his lips to imprison hers in a hard kiss.

'That's better,' he said, drawing away to look down on her, his eyes dark and smouldering. 'Perhaps now I can make myself heard.'

'How dare you!' she gasped, her breathing rapid and harsh. 'How dare you assault me like this . . .'

'If you keep on wriggling this way, you are asking for trouble!' he rebuked her sharply and, raising himself still further to look down on her almost naked breast, remarked, 'Your appearance is extremely provocative—any man would be tempted . . .'

'Then forget it!' she snapped, shrugging the strap of her slip on to her shoulder, her cheeks aflame with embarrassment, 'and let me go, immediately!'

Loosening his grip slightly, he smiled, and on a dry note said, 'It's a pity you didn't enjoy being kissed, it was the only way I knew of keeping you quiet. And perhaps now you have learned that anger can lead to passion— though if you lashed Thorpe so soundly with your tongue, I would have thought you knew that already!'

'What are you suggesting?' she demanded indignantly, managing to free one hand to adjust her slip and cover the expanse of bare flesh his eyes had just devoured. 'Let me tell you, I have never been in a situation such as this before, and I don't intend repeating it,' she finished, with a defiant lift of her chin. 'Right now, I'm going to dress and leave, and I don't care where I spend the night. Anything would be better than this!'

His eyes narrowing, Luis increased his hold on her. 'It appears I shall have to silence you yet again,' he warned, 'and I don't object to the task one little bit!'

'You wouldn't!' she began but, seeing his determined expression, felt it wiser to hold her tongue. 'Please, Luis, will you let me go now?' she begged him softly, hoping to appeal to his better nature. 'You're hurting my arm,'

He released his grip and, taking her hands, he gave an apologetic smile. 'Forgive me,' he said gently, his thumb caressing the reddened patch on her slim wrist. 'I didn't mean to hurt you, I merely wanted to explain my presence. It really is my bedroom . . .'

'But I saw you put your cases in the next room, and I was sure you indicated this door,'

'Next door is my dressing room and I dispensed with the bed to make room for a desk,' he explained. 'And, like you, I was tired and needed a rest. If you will just be sensible about it, do you think I would have remained fully dressed if I had had other intentions? After all, it should be quite in order for me to take a siesta with my fiancée—no?'

Noting he was fully clothed, apart from his jacket and shoes, Kate gave a long sigh. 'I wish you wouldn't call me your fiancée.'

He smiled and, raising her hand to his lips, said confidently, 'I think you will grow to like me in time,' and, rising from the bed, added, 'I don't usually meet with so much opposition,' before he went from the room.

Open-mouthed with amazement, Kate stared after him, her heart pounding madly in her breast. Really, this man was the limit! She should have rushed from the room screaming hysterically; the normal reaction of any girl who found a man in her bed uninvited. Yet she had experienced a feeling of embarrassed surprise rather than the terrifying shock one would have expected in this situation.

'Damn you!' she swore under her breath, yet she knew that for as long as she needed the shelter he offered, she'd have to curb her tongue so as not to arouse the oppressive instincts of the Spaniard. Perhaps it would be safer to play an altogether different role—one quite foreign to her nature—of the helpless little female, totally reliant on his superior knowledge and strength.

Still deep in thought, Kate started when the door opened a few inches and her suitcase was pushed through; 'Thought you might need something out of here,' Luis' voice came from the other side of the door. 'And if you would like to take a shower, it is through the adjoining room—so please help yourself.'

'Thank you, I will,' Kate called as the door closed and, opening her case, took out a change of underwear, a pair of fawn cotton trousers and matching jacket. Placing them on the bed, she took her bag of toiletries into the next room where she noticed the desk Luis had mentioned and, opposite, a line of fitted wardrobes with a long mirror on the centre door. The adjoining bathroom was tiled in a beautiful shade of blue and matching towels hung on the rails. And on the shelf above, she saw an array of bottles and jars; after-shave and talc of purely masculine choice. Once undressed, she turned on the well-equipped

50

shower, luxuriating in the scented bath gel and refreshing water.

With a large bath towel draped around her, tucked in under the arms, she gathered up her clothes and unlocked the bathroom door. But, just as she was closing it behind her, she saw Luis' reflection in the long mirror as he entered the room from the hall. With a startled sound she hesitated, the clothes she was carrying slipping to the floor. For a moment he merely stared until a slow smile spread over his face and he took a step towards her.

'Go away!' she shrieked, gathering the towel more closely around her, and drew in a quick breath when he continued to advance her way.

Shooting her a mocking glance, he stooped to retrieve her fallen clothing and said a trifle impatiently, 'Surely we're not going through all that again? Here, take your belongings and go and get dressed before I am further tempted to silence you.'

'You wouldn't dare!' she muttered, reaching out to retrieve her clothes.

'Wouldn't I?' he challenged, one dark brow raised as he surveyed her with interest. 'Just try me!'

Knowing he may well act upon his challenge, Kate bit back a sharp retort, taking a hurried step forward to snatch the clothes from his hand just when she felt the towel begin to slip from her body.

With one quick movement he flung her clothes on a nearby chair and came towards her, grasping both ends of the bath towel together in one strong hand. 'If you are wise you will get dressed quickly and another word from you and I will drag this towel away,' he threatened, his dark eyes glittering under long lashes as he towered over her. 'It would be so easy!'

'If you are waiting to use the shower, I'll go . . .' Kate began, her trepidation increasing as, with gentle fingers, he deftly tucked the towel around her again.

'Actually, I just came in for a change of clothes as there is another bathroom at the end of the hall. If we hadn't bumped into each other like this, I would have been ready by now.'

'S-sorry if I've delayed you.' she apologised in a faintly tremulous voice.

'Do I detect a hint of acid in your tone?' he queried as he opened the wardrobe door and selected a light suit.

'Of course not. I merely thought you'd be in a hurry to get away.'

'Yes, I do think it a good idea if we dine a little earlier than usual. It will give you a chance to see the city at night . . .'

'Dine?' Kate broke in. 'But I don't expect you to take me to dinner.'

'Why not? You must eat,' he said

pleasantly. 'But if you are still tired after your journey, I won't keep you out late, I promise.'

They dined in an exclusive restaurant situated in a fashionable quarter where it soon became obvious to her that Luis was a well-respected customer. The head waiter, resplendent in a tail suit, preceded them to a table where, once he had ensured they were comfortably seated, he gave his full attention to Luis who immediately engaged him in rapid conversation.

On hearing her own name, Kate glanced up just as the waiter turned his attention her way. And, taking her hand, he bowed deeply, his face wreathed in smiles.

'What did he say?' Kate enquired after the waiter had taken their order. 'He spoke so quickly, I couldn't catch a thing.'

'He was merely expressing his delight when I told him we are celebrating,' Luis replied with a humorous quirk of his lips.

'Celebrating?' Kate began, with a puzzled frown. 'But I thought I heard my name mentioned. Oh, no! You didn't tell him I am your fiancée?'

'Why not?' Luis looked surprised. 'He was delighted.'

'Oh Luis!' She gave a sigh of exasperation. 'You've got to stop playing games.' She checked herself; it just wasn't worth arguing with him again and by this time tomorrow she would have bade him farewell.

'This is no game, Katherine, I am quite serious. I have much to offer—a sound reputation, respectable family background and, unlike your friend Thorpe, cheating has never been my line of business.'

'Must you bring him into conversation!' she exclaimed crossly. 'And please stop talking about marriage, you know it annoys me.'

'Really, Katherine,' he rebuked her mockingly, 'if you are going to be angry with me I shall have to deal with you—yes, even here,' he added softly, seeing her defiant expression.

Kate suffered the remainder of her meal in silence, knowing full well that to remind him of her rights would merely tempt him to carry out his threat. But when the waiter came to their table bearing champagne to celebrate the occasion, his presence compelled her to break her silence and utter a few complimentary remarks on the high quality of service and the delicious food Luis had selected from the menu.

Avoiding Luis' direct gaze for some time after that, Kate felt quite guilty when, with what seemed genuine concern, he remarked, 'You are very quiet, Katherine, are you tired?'

'Yes, Luis,' she agreed hastily, 'perhaps I am. I'm sorry.'

'Don't apologise,' He smiled, rising to withdraw her chair and, as they left the restaurant, added, 'You have had a very trying time recently but you will soon recover,'

Warmed by his concern, Kate allowed him to take her hand again as they strolled back to his car. But her feeling of contentment was soon shattered when he helped her into the car, saying, 'We'll save the late night out until you are rested and have unpacked something more suitable to wear. That outfit is anything but flattering.'

'How do you mean, suitable?' she demanded a trifle sharply as he slid into the driving seat. 'And what's wrong with what I'm wearing?'

'You should wear something more feminine —definitely not trousers.'

'If you prefer frills, then I'm afraid you're going to be disappointed. I like something much more practical!'

'How typically English,' he countered scornfully. 'You look like Miss Prim, the office typist.'

'I see,' she responded coolly, fighting to restrain her rising anger.

'I see,' he mimicked. 'Again that typically cool English reserve,'

'Perhaps it's because I am English!' she flared. 'And what gives you the right to criticise me—you don't own me.'

Glancing sideways, he gave a slow smile. 'Not yet,' came his soft reply. 'I can't wait to see you in a pretty dress, one that will show off your legs, instead of that hideous garment you are wearing now,'

Though inwardly seething with rage, somehow Kate managed to ignore his insulting remark and when the car pulled up outside his apartment she almost wept with relief.

'Don't bother to get out,' she said as he pulled on the brake. 'If you hand me the key I can open the door myself.'

'I wouldn't dream of allowing you to do it yourself,' he said indignantly, alighting from the car. But before he got round to the passenger door, Kate was already standing on the pavement, waiting to wish him good-night.

'Let us have another coffee,' he suggested, inserting the key in the lock. 'And I may also have a brandy before I turn in.'

Sighing resignedly, Kate followed him to the lift. Perhaps he'd drink his coffee quickly, then leave, if she feigned extreme tiredness. It had been too much to hope this chivalrous Spaniard would leave her on the doorstep before going on his way, but if she yawned convincingly he should take the hint and go.

In the apartment he showed her the kitchen and explained how he made the coffee, leaving her to the task while he went to pour himself a brandy. But, when she took the tray into the sala, her spirits sank—he had poured two drinks and now lay back in an arm chair, completely relaxed.

'Thank you, but I don't think I want

another drink,' she refused politely. 'Just coffee is fine for me.'

'Come, the night is young,' he smiled persuasively, rising to take the tray. 'And we have much to discuss.'

'Can't it wait until tomorrow? I'm dreadfully tired, and I wouldn't have thought it wise to have another drink when you're driving.'

'Driving?' he queried, shooting her a curious look. 'Why should I worry about that?'

'Suit yourself,' she said with an indifferent shrug, 'but I'd rather not talk tonight.'

'Then tomorrow it shall be,' he agreed amiably. 'But before you retire I will collect anything I need from the dressing room. I couldn't bear being subjected to the sight of your near-naked body twice in one day!'

'Oh, I'll wait to retire until after you have left.'

'Left?' he queried, with an amused gaze. 'My dear Katherine, I intend sleeping here tonight!'

CHAPTER THREE

It was a moment before Kate found her voice after Luis divulged his plans. 'Sleep here?' she finally managed in a strangled tone. 'But you never said anything about this before. '

'Really, Katherine,' he broke in impatiently, 'you didn't expect me to leave you alone here, did you?'

'Why not? I'm not the nervous type and quite used to being on my own so there is no need for you to stay on my account. In any case, won't your family be expecting you? They could be anxious if you don't arrive home.'

He cocked an eyebrow at her derisively. 'Like you, Katherine, I do not have to account for my movements, so there is no need for you to worry your pretty little head about my family. Providing the business is going well they make no demands on my time.' Then, with a hint of a smile, he added, 'Surely, we are now acquainted well enough for you not to fear spending another night under my roof?'

'Y-yes, I suppose so,' she stammered meekly, her confidence ebbing. It was not that she feared he may take advantage of her by force, rather she may be rendered unable to resist his tantalising persuasion. She had fought against him when he had endeavoured to silence her, yet had enjoyed the sensation he had evoked when he succeeded. And she had to take a deep, calming breath before continuing, 'But there is only one bed.'

'I intend sleeping here,' he assured her promptly, indicating the large settee. 'A blanket and pillow are all I shall require.'

'You make me feel quite guilty. Will you be comfortable?'

'Quite frankly, I would prefer my own bed,' he said, then paused and, with a meaningful look continued, 'unless you are willing to share, I have no alternative. However, should your pangs of guilt become too painful to bear, give me a call and I will soothe them,' he teased gently and bent to place a light kiss on her cheek. 'Sleep well. You can rest assured I shall not enter your room unless you call.'

'I hope I can rely on that,' she returned crisply then, seeing his eyes darken, murmured a hurried, 'Good night,' and left the room.

Once alone, Kate let out a sighing breath and sank to the bed. She was convinced Luis would keep his promise yet she'd had to have the last word, provoking him. The completely unexplainable effect he had upon her usually composed manner was beyond her. Initially, she had been quite alarmed to learn he intended to stay the night though, deep down, she was glad he wasn't leaving and, reluctantly, had to admit to herself that the

59

briefness of his parting kiss had left her feeling empty inside.

*   *   *

Kate awoke to realise the shrill cry of terror had just died on her own parted lips. She had been dreaming—the train had crashed—but she quickly ascertained the deafening crack had come from outside when a flash of blue lit up the entire room to remind her of her surroundings. Another roll of thunder sounded overhead like none she had experienced, before and her hand flew to her throat as she uttered a startled gasp and heard Luis call her name.

When she didn't immediately respond, Luis came into the room, his expression of concern clearly visible when lightning flashed again.

'Katherine!' he exclaimed as he came towards the bed. 'Are you frightened of the storm?'

Kate's reply was lost in a fresh crack of thunder, startling her further; when he reached out to take her hands.

'Darling you are terrified!' he exclaimed softly, drawing her close as he sank down on the bed beside her. 'Until you called out I didn't realise you would be so frightened by the storm.'

Calmed by his presence, Kate gave a shaky little laugh. 'I'm sorry, Luis at first I didn't

60

realise it was thunder, it seemed like the whole house was crashing around me. I didn't mean to disturb you,' she apologised, easing herself from his firm embrace, 'but I've never before heard thunder like this—it's terrifying!'

'My dear Katherine, don't apologise, you disturb me whether you intend to or not. However, I don't wish to complain as I enjoy comforting you. Our storms can be quite violent but they soon pass . . .'

'Like your moods,' she interjected smartly, attempting to quell the growing excitement caused by the closeness of his body and the smooth luxury of his silk robe against her skin.

Luis fell silent as another fierce crack of thunder rolled overhead causing Kate to tense in his arms, when he swiftly took possession of her lips. Fear of the raging storm faded from her mind and, dazed by his kiss, she was hardly aware of the loud knocking on the apartment door. Eventually, through her reeling senses she found strength to protest at the closeness of his embrace when the knocking grew louder as the thunder faded into the distance. 'Aren't you going, to see who it is?' she whispered when he didn't make a move.

Luis gave a muffled curse and tensed beside her. 'No, no' he murmured swiftly, 'I am not expecting anyone.'

'But it must be urgent, otherwise who would call on you in the middle of the night?'

'My dear Katherine, it is only half past eleven—hardly the middle of the night, especially in Spain.'   .

'I thought I had been asleep for hours!'

'Thirty minutes at the most, and now you can relax again, the worst of the storm has passed.'

'Then I no longer need you here to comfort me so you may as well answer the door,' she put in swiftly, easing herself away from him now that she was fully aware of her extremely vulnerable position.

The knocking on the outer door became more impatient and Luis laughed softly as he rose from the bed. 'But what if the storm returns?' he queried. 'I may choose to ignore you if you call my name a second time.'

'Call your name?' said Kate in surprise. 'I don't remember . . .'

'Ah but you did!' he cried triumphantly. 'Now tell me you don't desire my company tonight.'

A further spate of banging sent Luis quickly into the hall, leaving the bedroom door ajar and not bothering to put on the light.

'Marie-Louisa!' she heard him exclaim before a torrent of words spoken in a furious female voice drowned anything else he may have said.

Kate immediately presumed the caller to be an irate wife seeking out her erring husband and was horrified to think what action the woman may take if she found his bed occupied. Or, was it perhaps a distraught girlfriend with whom he should have kept an appointment that evening? Yet, Luis didn't behave like a guilty husband, or an apologetic boyfriend. In fact, he sounded faintly amused as he said in a lazy Spanish tongue, 'Can't you sleep?'

'Sleep!' the newcomer snorted. 'Can you sleep through such a storm?'

'Of course,' Luis responded convincingly. 'Now, what is it you require?'

'Can't you guess,' the woman snapped, 'or haven't you tried your lights during the last half hour?'

'No, I haven't,' Luis admitted, and Kate heard the click of a switch. 'Actually, I was in bed, but if you wait one moment I'll go and find the candles. One of these days my stock will run out—you shouldn't rely on me every time.'

'You don't usually retire so early—is someone else here?'

The woman's voice had taken on a suspicious tone, causing Kate to freeze as she was slipping on her lacy robe. She heard Luis laugh, flicking his lighter as he moved in the direction of the kitchen. And, even though Kate's knowledge of Spanish was limited, she knew sufficient to understand the caller was not unfamiliar to Luis and she hardly dared to breathe as the tap-tapping of high heels

63

advanced along the hall.

Now they had moved into the kitchen, their voices less audible. Curious as to whom the visitor could be, Kate drew the robe around her and tip-toed over to the slightly open door to take a peep. She saw Luis emerge from the kitchen and, clearly silhouetted in the flickering light of the candle he was carrying, the shapely figure of a young woman, her eyes riveted on the bedroom door.

The woman exclaimed sharply in Spanish, turning to Luis with an accusing stare, when Kate realised it was too late to draw back. Luis merely shook his head, his expression one of amusement as he said, 'Marie-Louisa, you should have been a detective. Stop being so dramatic and come and meet Katherine Shaw, an English girl who travelled with me from Paris. I offered her shelter until her uncle arrives in Barcelona—he has been delayed by the airport strike.'

Kate gave an apprehensive smile as Luis made the introduction, too embarrassed to step forward to take the woman's hand.

'Marie-Louisa is a relative of mine and lives in the apartment above,' Luis explained lighting a second candle and placing it in an ashtray on the hall table. 'She came down for candles as the electricity is off due to the storm. It's quite a common occurrence here— one flash of lightning and we're in darkness.' He laughed and passed another lighted candle to Kate.

'I imagine she was more than willing to accept your hospitality, Luis,' Marie-Louisa sneered in good English, her dark gaze raking Kate from head to toe.

Ignoring the other's undisguised contempt, Kate managed a smile. 'I'm sorry, señorita, I'm not fully dressed so I hope you won't mind if I close the door?'

'Mind? I think it is hilarious!' Marie-Louisa shrieked with laughter, her bracelets jangling as she gestured in Kate's direction. 'To discover an English girl dressed in virginal white in my cousin's bedroom contradicts all he would have me believe . . .'

'Marie-Louisa—enough!' Luis snapped, his dark eyes flashing. 'How dare you speak to a guest of mine like that!'

'Guest did you say? Pah! I consider her presence to be a warning of a forthcoming scandal, the second in your family, I believe?'

'It is no concern of yours!' Luis hissed, his voice carrying clearly into the bedroom as Kate closed the door and, in his own language, ended, 'You now have what you came for so, good-night!' And with that, the girl fell silent, only the thud of the front door and Luis' muffled curse a sign that she had left.

Even though it was still very hot in the room, Kate found herself trembling in the few moments silence following the departure of

Marie-Louisa. Then there came a tap on the door and Luis appeared, his expression slightly apprehensive as he said, 'I wish to apologise for the behaviour of my cousin—her remarks were unforgivable.'

'If you insist upon causing a scandal in the family . . .' Kate reminded him, adding with icy sweetness, 'though, obviously you have led Marie-Louisa to believe you lead a very pure life but what about *my* reputation?'

Luis uttered a sigh of impatience. 'Believe me, Katherine, your reputation is my concern, you are over-reacting. In any case, in this light Marie-Louisa wouldn't see you at all clearly so your reputation is safe.'

'If you had your way I wouldn't have one to save!' she retorted angrily. 'I think I owe your cousin a great deal—perhaps I should thank her for saving my virtue.'

Luis raised his brows and held her gaze. 'I do believe you are angry because of the interruption,' he suggested, a flicker of a smile playing round his sensuous mouth. 'Before all this you were soft and sweet in my arms and you wouldn't have given your reputation the slightest consideration if my stupid cousin had not arrived at such a precious moment.'

'Such conceit!' Kate snorted, 'you appear to be under the impression you are totally irresistible . . .'

He held up his hand to silence her. 'The sole object of my visit was to apologise for my

66

cousin,' he reminded her. 'If she was other than a member of my family I would ignore her presence. As it is, I must suffer her whims and tantrums if only for the sake of her mother—a task I find most irksome at times.' He shrugged and, with a most appealing expression, added, 'I can do no more than apologise in the hope that you do not hold me responsible for her unforgivable remarks.'

Kate gave a long sigh, her anger ebbing as she realised Luis accepted full responsibility for his cousin's behaviour. 'You were very tolerant—it must be difficult.'

'Then am I correct in assuming we are forgiven?'

'Of course,' she agreed softly.

'I expect the electricity supply will be back to normal by the morning,' he assured her pleasantly and, putting down the candle, turned on his heels and left the room.

Kate had taken an involuntary step back, convinced Luis was going to kiss her and now experienced a slight pang of annoyance over his swift departure. Silently reproaching herself, she slid into bed; all was quiet again but for an occasional drip of water from the eaves. It was as though the storm had affected their emotions; thunder and torrential rain had aroused an anger which was replaced by a calmer understanding once the storm abated.

After breakfast the following morning, Luis reminded her of his suggested visit to Sagrada

Familia made the previous day.

'You hadn't forgotten?' he asked, noting her lack of enthusiasm. 'I realise you will not relax until this relative of yours arrives, that is if I can assume he really is your uncle?'

'Of course he is!' she bristled. 'Do you imagine I would take advantage of your hospitality whilst I wait for my boyfriend, or whatever you would call him . . . really!'

'Ah, Katherine, forgive me, I had reckoned without the strong feelings of justice you English possess. If you prefer to remain indoors, I am sure we can think of some way to pass the time—si?'

'The purpose of my visit to Barcelona was to meet my uncle, not to provide a source of entertainment for some arrogant Spanish wine merchant!' she retaliated. 'I think it's time I returned to the hotel . . .'

'And if I had not been so concerned about the welfare of a visitor to my country—a particularly naïve one at that—I would have left you there yesterday,' he cut in, 'so save your abuse, it is not very becoming!'

'Oh, you're insufferable!' Kate gasped. 'And it has occurred to me that the message you read aloud yesterday could have been anything you wanted it to be—a means of persuading me to come here.'

With a mirthless smile he advanced slowly towards her, his arms extended as he said, 'A little late in coming to that conclusion, are you

68

not?' and, taking her firmly by the shoulders, continued, 'Katherine, you little fool, can you not see, if I had wanted to take advantage of you in some way I would have done so before now.'

'I suppose so,' she admitted reluctantly, shrugging him away and closing her eyes in an attempt to fight back the tears that threatened to overwhelm her.

Looking down on her Luis gave a rueful smile. 'Actually, I have been rather unfair,' he admitted. 'I rang Malaga earlier and was told the first plane arrives in Barcelona at mid-day, so we have plenty of time. I was going to surprise you but I realise now you are hardly in the mood.'

Gathering her composure, Kate agreed to the outing he suggested which was within walking distance of his apartment. The morning air was fresh after the storm, compared with the heavy atmosphere of the previous evening, and Kate enjoyed walking along the streets which were bathed in sunlight.

Taking her hand when they needed to cross the traffic-filled streets, Luis was soon pointing up to the spires of the cathedral which now towered above them, and suggested they circle the building before going inside.

Kate gazed up in awe at the unusual monumental façades and the towers topped by attractive mosaics. At the Birth façade she was truly captivated and found it difficult to tear herself away.

'There's so much to see!' she exclaimed in delight as they neared the entrance. And, once inside, she was again surprised to see it was unfinished.

Luis laughed. 'You didn't expect such a masterpiece still to be in the midst of its building programme, did you?'

Watching the huge blocks of stone being lifted into place by tall cranes, Kate nodded. 'I wonder when it will be completed—do you know?'

'I can not say, but I expect it will be many years. You know . . .' he added thoughtfully, 'when I think of it, it has grown considerably in my lifetime.'

Kate was fascinated by the building and they wandered around for almost an hour when he reminded her of the passing time.

'If you would like to see more, we can return another day,' he promised. 'Barcelona has many works of Gaudi design; we shall see them all in time.'

'But perhaps I shall be too busy to sightsee during my stay,' she pointed out. 'Though I must admit I've enjoyed all this immensely, but I intend to do some work whilst I'm here.'

'You must have some time off—grape picking can be back-breaking work.'

'I must earn my keep!' She laughed. 'I shall

feel as though I am on holiday, otherwise.'

'Then you can make coffee for us—how's that?' he offered and, taking her hand, they strolled back to his apartment.

Kate was pouring coffee when the telephone rang, and it wasn't long before Luis announced her uncle would be in Barcelona before lunch.

'He managed to secure a seat on the first flight out,' he told her. 'Had he been obliged to take a train he would not have reached here until late evening. He rang the hotel a short while ago and the receptionist has been most efficient and helpful on this occasion.'

'I expect it was the generous tip you gave him,' she laughed. 'You have gone to a lot of trouble on my account and I'm very grateful.'

'Will you miss me, Katherine?' Luis asked unexpectedly as he seated himself beside her on the settee.

'Yes, naturally,' she managed a trifle hesitantly, 'you have been very kind.'

'Then this is not a kiss goodbye,' he said, then taking her cup and saucer from her hand, he kissed her gently on the mouth and drew away smiling.

Kate experienced a curious tingle of pleasure as Luis kissed her and, endeavouring to inject a little calm into her voice, suggested it was time for her to leave for the hotel.

'I will drive you there,' Luis offered, rising from his seat.

'I could get a taxi,' she offered, 'less bother for you.'

'Certainly not. I prefer to take you myself and ensure you arrive safely.'

Suppressing her indignation, Kate allowed him to drive her to the hotel where he helped her in with her luggage before presenting himself at reception to confirm her uncle's time of arrival.

'Señor Shaw arrived a few minutes ago,' he assured her. 'And I have requested a porter take up your case.' Then drawing a visiting card from his pocket, he added, 'My telephone number—you may need it.'

Kate was impressed by the efficient manner he handled everything yet, at the thought of him leaving, she was suddenly overcome by a wave of despair.

'Before you go . . .' she began, her voice wavering as she strove to find the right words. 'Oh, Luis, I am really grateful and I hope you will ignore what I said earlier . . .' She hesitated as Luis put his finger to his lips to silence her.

'Perhaps we should leave this conversation until another time,' he whispered. 'I see a gentleman advancing this way who could be a relative of yours.'

Kate turned just as Clive Shaw spoke her name and caught her in a welcoming embrace. 'Kate, my dear, it's good to see you. I've been more than a little worried not finding you here. You did arrive yesterday? The porter mentioned something . . .'

'Don't worry, I'll tell you about that later. First, let me introduce you to Luis, or rather, Señor Vendrell who has been a great help to me since I arrived.'

As the two men shook hands, Kate made an effort to compose herself. And when her uncle suggested they all took coffee in the lounge, the awful sense of finality which had threatened began to subside. Suddenly realising Luis was speaking, she dragged her thoughts back to the present.

'Hey, Kathcrine,' he said pleasantly, 'I was enquiring if you would like me to explain the latest developments? I realise it is not my business, but I know it will be unpleasant for you to reap over the details a second time.'

Kate nodded and followed the men into the lounge. Her arrival in Paris had been a nightmare and she was grateful to Luis for sparing her the need to go over it again. In a kind of daze she heard Luis disclose what had happened concerning John Thorpe and, even though he gave only a modest account of the part he had played, he managed to convey quite clearly just how difficult it would have been for her to manage without him.

'My goodness, Kate, it was extremely fortunate you met Señor Vendrell,' Clive Shaw exclaimed when Luis had finished speaking. 'At least you still have the contracts

73

so I can telephone many of the vineyards and warn them of the possibility of Thorpe calling. I'm positive it's his reason for being in Spain.' He sighed and shook his head. 'I was a fool to think he would give up so easily and, although I don't like the idea of bringing in the police, I may have no alternative.'

'I think you should have done that in the first place,' Luis remarked, though not unkindly, 'but I suppose you were in a difficult position then, having Katherine's feelings to take into account.'

'Ah, but I don't have that worry now Kate has turned him down,' Clive said with a smile of satisfaction. 'Maybe she told you he once proposed marriage?'

'Yes, Katherine did mention it,' Luis agreed, 'though I am sure she is now fully recovered.' Shooting her a sideways glance, he continued, 'In fact, we have become quite good friends in the short time we have been acquainted—indeed, quite good.'

'Pleased to hear it, Señor Vendrell,' Clive responded agreeably. 'She's an intelligent girl—maybe a bit headstrong at times—needs a firm hand, if you know what I mean?' He ended on a jocular note, much to Kate's annoyance.

'Exactly what I have told her myself,' Luis agreed, giving Kate a meaningful look.

'Anyone would think you two were discussing a thoroughbred horse!' Kate

74

intervened with a short laugh. 'Besides, I find it rather embarrassing to be the object of your discussion so, if you will excuse me, I'll go and unpack. Thank you again Luis, I am most grateful . . .'

'Don't make it sound so final,' Clive broke in as Luis rose to take Kate's hand. 'I would like to meet you again, señor. Perhaps you would join us for dinner?'

Whilst Clive Shaw had been speaking, Luis caught her eye and, with an almost devilish gleam in his, said, 'I will look forward to that, it won't be such a wrench if I see you both later.' And with a slight inclination of his dark head he promised to return at nine o'clock.

With her clothes hung neatly away, Kate allowed herself the luxury of a siesta and it was the shrill tone of the telephone beside the bed which awoke her. And when the receptionist announced there was a call for her, she sat up quickly, thinking it was Luis.

'Yes, this is Katherine Shaw,' she replied, excitement welling up inside her. But when she realised the caller was John Thorpe she froze and, before she could replace the receiver, he spoke again.

'Don't cut me off, Kate, I want to apologise . . .'

'You—apologise?' she began, her heart starting to pound. 'I don't wish to hear . . .'

'Please, Kate, hear me out,' he pleaded, 'I realise I shouldn't have said what I did the

75

other day, and I'm sorry.'

'I don't want to hear any more . . .' Kate managed but he broke in again.

'Kate, please—I always thought you a fair-minded girl—can't you understand, I was jealous, but now I realise it was wrong of me.'

'It most certainly was!'

'I know, and I'm sorry, believe me, and I want to put things right.'

'Forget it, John,' Kate cut in, quickly replacing the receiver.

Determined to push John's call to the back of her mind, Kate took a shower and prepared herself for the evening before going to join her uncle, which gave them plenty of time to discuss his plans.

Promptly at nine Luis entered the lounge where Kate and her uncle were comfortably seated, sipping an aperitif. He had changed into a dark suit which accentuated his strong, lean frame as he advanced their way with almost cat-like grace. He smiled, accepting Clive's invitation to join them when he let his gaze fall slowly over Kate, his eyes coming to rest on the hemline of the light blue dress she wore.

'You look extremely pretty tonight, Katherine,' Luis smiled. 'A compliment to us gentlemen.'

'Indeed, and we had a long rest this afternoon,' Clive put in, 'also a good discussion about our business plans.'

'Plans?' Luis queried, glancing from one to the other. 'May I ask what they are, Señor Shaw?'

'Please, call me Clive,' the older man said. 'Kate does, and as I consider her almost a partner in business, I prefer it. Now, about those plans we have been discussing. I want Kate to learn more about the quality of wine, so she needs to understand the process of wine production. I am going to make enquiries of my customers to ask if they will allow her to stay with them during the harvest. It should give her a good insight in preparation for next season.'

Kate leaned forward in her chair. 'Hey, just a moment. When we discussed this you didn't say anything about it being this year. Why the sudden decision?'

'It's obvious, you're already here so we might as well take the opportunity.'

'We?' she queried, her lips curving in a smile. 'I am the only one in need of instruction, though I didn't expect it so soon.'

'I know, but a couple of months ago you didn't expect to make this journey. As you have ...'

'Clive Shaw!' Kate exclaimed laughingly. 'You're a very determined man!'

'A family trait, possibly?' Luis remarked. 'You know, strength of character. You must have worked extremely hard to keep the business going.'

'Damned hard!' Clive agreed. 'When Kate's father died, I had to rely on her help to keep the place going. Have you got parents behind you, Luis?'

'My father, though he leaves the managing to me.'

'And is your mother involved . . .?' Kate began, only to have her question brushed aside when Luis indicated there was a table awaiting them.

Dinner was a leisurely and enjoyable meal and, as it progressed, Kate found herself wondering how she could ever have considered Luis to be anything but a delightful companion. He chatted amiably with her uncle; the main topic of conversation being of vines and grapes, their quality and type, to perfecting conditions of storage in the cellars.

'I'm quite looking forward to my course of tuition in the vineyards,' Kate announced eagerly as the waiter served their final course. 'I was aware of a considerable variety of grape, and perhaps I shall learn to recognise some by their taste.'

Clive and Luis regarded her bright-eyed enthusiasm smilingly, and Kate saw just how happy her uncle appeared in the company of the dark Spaniard; they shared a professional interest which she also aspired to possess.

'Then why not start immediately—well, within the next few days?' Luis suggested and, with a relaxed air of charm and authority, offered, 'I can give you all the instruction you need. There is ample room for you at the villa and, as harvest is soon to begin, it couldn't have been a more suitable time. Come back with me tomorrow, there is no point in you staying here alone.'

Kate experienced a great wave of relief. Although she had kept a cheerful façade throughout the evening, thoughts of John had marred her inner pleasure. At Luis' villa she would be safe. John couldn't contact her there.

CHAPTER FOUR

'I would have preferred more time to look round the city,' Kate remarked as she and her uncle sat down to breakfast the following morning. 'After all, it is my first visit.'

'You'll have plenty of time for sightseeing when the harvest is over.' Clive Shaw laughed. 'The grapes won't wait for you to have a shopping spree; picking will start any day now.'

'But I need to buy new clothes; I have nothing suitable to wear at dinner.'

'And you want to impress Luis,' he put in. 'Am I correct?'

'Of course not!' Kate spluttered, her coffee cup clattering on the saucer. 'It's just that my clothes are so unsuitable for this climate . . .'

'I liked the dress you wore at dinner last night, and I noticed Luis eyed you most favourably,' Clive chuckled. 'Yes, he's got his eye on you, my girl, that's for sure!'

'Oh, you're impossible! I have only known the man for two days.'

'Even so, you have made quite an impression upon him, and I'm sure he'd like to see you in a pretty dress rather than trousers.'

'Men,' Kate grumbled, 'you're all alike! And that is the only suitable dress I have with me so I'll have to do some shopping before I go.'

'Well, finish your breakfast and I'll take you to some of the best fashion shops in town. Luis isn't calling for you until after lunch, so you have plenty of time.'

'All this rush!' Kate sighed, though secretly glad of the opportunity to further her wardrobe before she was to visit Luis' home. Even though she objected to his rather dictatorial manner at times, she was inwardly delighted at the prospect of spending more time in his company before the day came for her to leave Spain. She would have at least two weeks, Clive had informed her the previous day. And he would be visiting other wine regions to complete his business transactions, enabling their company to build up sufficient stocks for the following year.

*   *   *

Kate was wearing one of her earlier purchases, a crisp yellow cotton dress, when Luis called at her hotel that afternoon and his eyes swept over her admiringly as she came from the lift, her uncle beside her.

'Good afternoon, Clive, Katherine,' he greeted, taking her cases. 'I trust you have had a comfortable stay?'

'Very comfortable,' Clive agreed, 'but now I must get to business. I've arranged for a hired

81

car to take me to the Rioja region. I could be away for almost a week, but I've got your telephone number, Luis, so I will call you on my return.'

'Perfect,' said Luis pleasantly. 'So, if you are ready, Katherine, we will leave right away.'

'She's ready, and delighted to be going with you, Luis. Take good care of her until I get back.'

'Of course. I will treat her as one of the family.' Luis smiled, adding, 'and there is something I wish to discuss with you when next we meet.'

'Anything important?' Clive asked, studying Luis' expression, 'or will it keep?'

'I consider it important,' Luis replied, 'but it will wait.'

Kate felt the blood rush to her cheeks and, after a hasty farewell to Clive, she tackled Luis about his last remark as they went to his car.

'This teasing,' she began accusingly, 'it is embarrassing for me. You know, this marriage business you keep hinting at.'

'Actually, I was referring to Thorpe,' he said casually as they drove away. 'Only this morning I heard he had approached a local vineyard, but it appears Clive had forewarned the owner and I meant to congratulate him on his quick move.'

'Oh,' Kate said, feeling utterly foolish under his penetrating gaze. 'I'm sorry, I didn't realise, Clive never mentioned it.'

'No, but now you have reminded me,' he began teasingly, 'we will see how you behave in the next few days.'

'As a guest in your house I shall behave with the utmost dignity,' she shot back indignantly.

'How disappointing,' he mocked, casting her a sideways glance.

'I shall at least consider your family.'

'Yes, my aunt is inclined to keep a sharp eye on things at home and, although she is not involved in the vineyard, she has been very loyal to the family since her husband, my father's brother, died many years ago.'

'And she prefers to live in your home?'

'Here, it is the duty of the family to provide for her. She has never considered having a home of her own whereas her daughter, Marie-Louisa, prefers an apartment in town.'

Being reminded of Marie-Louisa gave Kate a start and she was relieved to learn it was unlikely they would meet again. One such encounter was enough.

'I expect she enjoys city life,' Kate remarked as they left the bustling streets to take a road out of the city. 'How far to your home?'

'Only another eight kilometres and we're there,' Luis informed her as he increased his speed.

As the tension eased out of their conversation, Kate relaxed, absorbing the scenery as they drove farther into the country where unfamiliar trees grew at the roadside. Cypress sheltered a church surrounded by a high walled burial ground. Clusters of houses clung to the distant hillsides, their shutters closed to the strong afternoon sun. They passed over parched riverbeds deeply cracked by the heat, and soon row upon row of vines came into view, weighted down by grapes just ready to be picked.

Luis had opened the roof of the car and now the warm scented air lifted her spirits as they drove along narrowing roads. Glancing sideways, he smiled, his warm brown eyes crinkling at the corners as he gestured towards the adjoining land.

'These are my vines,' he stated proudly, 'and they are laden with fruit of excellent quality.'

'Sounds to me as though you really enjoy your work,' Kate commented, noticing his expression as he observed his crops with pride.

'Yes, I do, but it is very hard work. It has been my life since I was a child when I could hardly bear the waiting for school holidays at this time of the year. I longed to be in the vineyards with my father.'

Kate smiled. This side of Luis' character had such natural charm and she said pleasantly, 'You never told me anything about your mother. Was she also involved?'

For a long moment he didn't reply and Kate

saw his expression change.

'That is all in the past,' he said finally, then fell silent as they turned off the road into a tree-lined avenue.

Beyond the trees, Kate saw a large old house the colour of sand. 'Is this your home?' she asked, amazed by its size and the spacious walled gardens in which it stood.

'Yes, we are home,' he agreed, his expression brightening again as he brought the car to a standstill inside the wrought iron gate.

'How delightful!' she breathed, remaining in her seat for a few moments to admire the view. 'I'm sure I shall enjoy being here.'

Luis merely smiled and came round the car to help her alight. It was only as they walked towards the main door that he paused, saying, 'I expect everyone is resting at present, but should we meet my aunt don't be surprised if she appears rather cool in her manner towards you. She finds it difficult to adjust to strangers in the house.'

'Don't worry,' Kate assured him. 'I can manage a greeting in Spanish so that should break the ice.'

Luis shrugged as though to dismiss the matter and, taking her cases from the boot, led her indoors.

'First, I will show you to your room,' he offered as they paused in the dimly lit hall, 'and then, unless you wish to rest, we can have

85

a cool drink on the patio.'

'Just a moment while I take all this in,' Kate begged, placing a restraining hand on his arm as her eyes travelled over the glossy marble floor to the carved ceiling where a huge crystal chandelier hung from its centre. 'It's really beautiful!' she exclaimed, her face wreathed in smiles.

'You like it?' he asked, his head held proudly erect as he followed her gaze. 'It will give me much pleasure to share my home with you for the next week or two.'

About to express her gratitude, Kate was suddenly aware they were not alone. Quickly dropping her hand from his arm, she raised her eyes to the wide staircase to see a woman standing on the landing, her features immobile as she watched from above.

'Ah, I see my aunt is not resting at the moment,' Luis said, 'come, I will introduce you.'

As they ascended the stairs, Kate met the stony gaze of his aunt who only directed her smiling attention to Luis when he made the introductions.

'Good afternoon, Señora Vendrell,' Kate managed in Spanish, a slight feeling of trepidation rising within her as she met the cold dark eyes of Luis' aunt.

'Good afternoon, Miss Shaw,' came the response, though she chose to ignore Kate's outstretched hand. 'I will show you to your room—Luis is very busy.'

Murmuring her thanks, Kate followed the slim, erect figure of Luis' aunt along the landing where, without a word, she flung open a door and indicated Kate should enter.

'It's a lovely room,' Kate complimented, 'and very kind of you to allow me to use it. I know I shall be comfortable here.'

'Is your interest in the grape harvest the sole reason for your visit?' the señora asked, without a flicker of emotion on her rather pale face.

'Of course,' Kate replied a trifle hesitantly. 'Why do you ask?'

Compressing her thin mouth, the señora ignored Kate's question and enquired, 'Exactly how long do you propose to stay?'

'Only a few days, until my uncle returns to Barcelona.'

'A few days, uh?' The señora frowned, causing Kate to feel rather uncomfortable.

'Yes, if that is convenient . . .' Kate began when the older woman swung sharply on her heel.

'Convenient?' she muttered. 'Pah!' And moving briskly away, she left Kate to stare after her in surprise.

With a shrug, Kate tried to dismiss the señora's cool manner and walked over to the window to open the shutters, allowing sunlight into the spacious room. Luis had warned her, she reminded herself, yet she felt increasingly unwelcome as she turned the matter over in her mind. Determined not to allow the woman's cool welcome to upset her, she started to unpack, admiring the large, carved mahogany wardrobe and chest of drawers as she hung up her clothes.

With her suitcase and holdall now empty, and everything neatly stored away, Kate made her way downstairs in search of Luis. The house seemed strangely quiet as she cautiously peered into the downstairs rooms and only when she walked out on to the patio did she see him lounging in a chair in the shade of a pittosporum tree at the end of a paved walk.

'Ah, Katherine!' he exclaimed, rising. 'I trust your room is to your liking?'

'Perfect, thank you,' she agreed, taking another chair, 'although I'm not sure your aunt is too happy about me being here.'

He shrugged, dismissively. 'It is just her way, don't let it worry you. Now, I will bring out drinks for us then we can discuss your programme. We shall have to work fast if you are to see the whole operation; the vineyard workers have already begun cutting the grapes, but today you shall rest to prepare yourself and I will explain the process.'

Luis went indoors, soon to return with a tray laden with jug and glasses. But, before he had set it down, his aunt had followed him across the patio.

'Luis, I will pour the drinks,' she offered unsmilingly. 'This is not man's work.'

Luis chuckled. 'I don't suppose Katherine would agree with that.'

'Maybe not,' Señora Vendrell agreed disparagingly, 'but she is English and they have very different ways, as I am sure you are already aware.'

The smile left Luis' face and he handed Kate a glass of sangria in silence.

'And why are you not resting, Luis?' his aunt asked, seating herself beside him. 'You have many hard days ahead of you now.'

'I am about to explain the process to Katherine and there is little time if she is to start work tomorrow,' he explained, a trifle impatiently.

'Miss Shaw is to work here!' the señora gasped in amazement. 'But it is no work for a woman—particularly an English woman . . .'

'She is already in the business,' Luis put in mildly, 'her family import wine.'

Señora Vendrell's mouth tightened and she returned her glass to the tray, untouched. 'And why choose this vineyard?' she asked, turning her cool gaze in Kate's direction. 'There are hundreds more in the area.'

'Quite by coincidence, really,' Kate explained. 'I met Luis on the train from Paris, then my uncle joined us in Barcelona and the idea came to us over dinner. My uncle is a buyer, you see, and he took me into the

89

business after my father died.' .

'You met on the train from Paris, did you say?' the señora asked, addressing Luis. 'A coincidence, of course?'

'Yes, and it was rather fortunate for us,' Luis told her. 'Katherine was in a position to warn us about a certain gentleman who could ruin our business. If you remember, earlier I told you about the man who called at the vineyard on the main road? They are new there so were glad of my warning and, of course, he will not sell to Thorpe when he needs to build up a reputable business.'

'Indeed, one must consider one's reputation,' his aunt agreed and, turning to Kate with an accusing stare, continued, 'So, it was you who stayed in Luis' apartment the other night?'

At that statement, Kate's colour rose and she glanced to Luis for support. 'Good gracious, Marie-Louisa has been quick with the news!' he exclaimed in mock surprise. 'If she was as good at her work she would go far.'

'Women of our breeding do not work for a living,' Señora Vendrell snorted, casting a disdainful glance at Kate. 'My daughter gives a little help with the books, but her future will be very different.'

'And it is for Katherine's future that I am explaining the business,' Luis put in, a devilish smile spreading across his face. 'I would like to think the future mistress of my home was

90

well acquainted with the work which is my whole life. Don't you agree?'

For a moment Señora Vendrell's expression was blank, then as his meaning penetrated her mind she tensed, her dark eyes fixed upon Kate.

'Mistress of your home—you mean . . . ?' she gasped as her hand flew to her throat. 'You can't mean . . . ?'

'He's teasing, señora,' Kate broke in, made uneasy by the other woman's icy stare and, appealing to Luis, said, 'Please, don't say such things.'

'You need not be shy, Katherine.' Luis smiled easily. 'People are bound to guess, sooner or later.'

'Really, Luis, you are behaving just like your father!' the señora snapped as she rose, going quickly into the house.

'Oh, Luis!' Kate said furiously, 'why must you insist upon embarrassing me this way? And you've upset your aunt too, quite unnecessarily.'

'She'll get used to the idea in time.' He smiled and reached for his glass.

'But I won't!' Kate objected. 'And if you're going to continue with this silly idea I can't possibly remain here!' she flared, rising from her chair.

'Hah, my wild beauty!' Luis exclaimed laughingly and, curling his long fingers round her wrist, drew her back to her seat. 'Let us not waste time, I have much to explain,' he continued, and went on to detail the process of wine making in such an interesting manner Kate was soon enthralled.

'You're making me feel quite impatient to get started,' Kate sighed happily. 'It all sounds so interesting.'

'You must wait until tomorrow,' Luis said, 'but today you can relax and enjoy yourself. I suggest you rest a while and join the family for dinner, later when it is a little cooler.'

'Yes, I think I shall rest now,' she said softly.

Kate dressed for dinner with the utmost care, choosing to wear a dress in the palest turquoise, bought in Barcelona only that morning. It was an expensive dress in soft chiffon, but Clive had been generous, saying, 'You need something rather special for your Mr Vendrell.'

My Mr Vendrell? she mused, what a ridiculous idea! But she loved the dress and swung round in front of the mirror so that the wide skirt floated out from just below her knee. She decided to fasten her fair curls on top of her head which showed the graceful lines of her neck to full advantage. Pleased with her appearance, she smiled at her reflection, yet asked herself why was she making such an effort to please a man who at times she almost hated?

Attempting to push her thoughts to the

back of her mind, she went downstairs to join the family at dinner and found Luis in the sitting room. But, seeing he was not alone she paused in the doorway until he came forward to greet her.

'My aunt and Marie-Louisa you already have met, so come and meet my father,' Luis invited, beckoning her towards the opposite end of the room, when Kate felt conscious of all eyes upon her, particularly those of Marie-Louisa who regarded her coldly. However, Luis' father had a gentle expression as he rose to greet her in a most courteous manner.

'Welcome to our home, Miss Shaw,' he said warmly in clear but heavily accented English and, taking her hand, motioned for her to be seated beside him.

Kate responded politely, adding how beautiful she thought the house, when she became aware of the exchanged glances of the two women present as Luis crossed to the cabinet to pour drinks.

It was only when Luis put a glass in her hand that she glanced up and caught his serious expression before he smiled, saying, 'My father enjoys a little conversation in English though he rarely has the opportunity to converse with anyone from that country these days.'

'Then you remember it well,' Kate complimented the older man. 'And I must improve my Spanish whilst I'm here.'

'Indeed you must,' Luis put in. 'Your business demands it,' he added smoothly, catching Kate's eye.

'Ah, yes, tell me about your family business,' Luis' father continued. 'I like to know what happens to our wines once they have left the cellars.'

Delighted by the older man's interest, Kate gave a brief account of the business in which, she and her uncle had now become involved. 'It's been jolly hard work since I lost my parents and my uncle needs a partner to take some of the responsibility from his shoulders,' she ended, taking an appreciative sip from her glass.

'It is tragic for one to be orphaned so young, but perhaps you will choose a husband who is suited to the work,' he smiled gently and, indicating that Luis should refill her glass, continued, 'I believe I met your father in London many years ago—a business meeting, of course.'

'And you remember him after all those years!' Kate exclaimed in pleasant surprise, adding sadly, 'It is almost four years since he died.'

'I am so sorry, child. I remember him particularly as a man of great integrity and, yes, you have his looks, not his colouring, but definitely, you are his daughter.'

'Really!' Señora Vendrell snorted derisively. 'How can my brother-in law possibly recall how the man looked after so many years?'

'And why not?' Señor Vendrell put in with a wry smile. 'I am not the senile old man you would have everyone believe. Miss Shaw's father stands out in my memory as a true English gentleman.'

'English gentleman!' sneered Marie-Louisa. 'I have yet to meet one . . .'

'You must forgive the ladies of my family,' Luis intervened. 'They have travelled little so do not have a true picture of foreigners other than the odd tourist here who hits the headlines.'

'I like the English,' Luis' father said, 'though I admit, in the past . . .'

'Don't you think it is time we went in for dinner, father?' Luis broke in, rather impolitely Kate thought, but noticed an almost wicked smile pass between the señora and her daughter as they rose to go into the dining room.

After dinner, they took coffee in the small lounge which overlooked the patio. The shutters were now drawn back and moths danced against the glass, attracted by the light.

Shortly after, the older man returned to his room and Luis also rose. 'I suggest you retire soon, Katherine as we must make an early start tomorrow. I'll see you at breakfast, seven thirty, and wear something sensible on your feet,' he added, noting her high-heeled sandals as he left the room.

Immediately the door closed behind him, Marie-Louisa said, 'I don't suppose you possess anything sensible to wear in the vineyards, do you?'

'Actually, I came well prepared for work,' Kate replied a trifle smugly, secretly glad she hadn't left behind all that Luis considered sensible.

'Not a very lady-like occupation,' Señora Vendrell remarked disparagingly. 'Here, only the working class are seen in the vineyards. The glamour is reserved for the ladies of the house, and Luis doesn't like the idea of women's independence; he would consider it most unfeminine.'

'I'm not trying to compete with Luis,' Kate replied tightly. 'I'm here purely in the interests of the trade. And, if you will excuse me, I think I will go to my room.'

Kate heard Marie-Louisa snigger as she closed the door behind her and felt rising anger towards the young woman. Or was this feeling of anger directed at Luis? Secretly, she had been anxious about being left alone with him this evening yet, now he had retired early, she felt piqued regarding his lack of attention.

Her thoughts continued to dwell on Luis as she undressed and climbed into bed, cascading unceasingly through her mind for almost another hour until she could no longer lie there in the stillness of the room. Rising, she slipped a wrap over her nightdress and

96

stepped out onto the balcony to stare up at the starlit sky.

From somewhere in the still warm night she heard the purr of an engine, then saw the lights of a car coming towards the villa. When the car came to a halt in the drive she drew back into the shadows in time to see Luis alight and heard the crunch of gravel as he walked in the direction of the house. A soft chuckle floated up from below, and a whispered, 'Sweet dreams, Katherine,' sent her hurriedly back into the room. Where could Luis have been at such a late hour, she wondered and, climbing back into bed, was soon fast asleep.

CHAPTER FIVE.

'You were waiting for me last night, were you not, Katherine?' Luis accused, a faintly mocking expression in his dark eyes. 'You have no need to reply, I can see by your expression.' He laughed. 'I caught sight of your white gown as I drove through the gate.

'Don't be ridiculous,' Kate denied. 'I was merely taking a breath of fresh air.'

'Were you nervous?' he asked with more concern. 'I was visiting a neighbouring vineyard but I wouldn't leave you alone in the house, if that is what troubles you.'

Kate hesitated then, spotting the manager of the vineyard approaching between the rows of vines, was thankful she need not reply.

'Ah, here is José!' Luis smiled, greeting the man in his local tongue before introducing Kate. José returned a formal welcome and the three of them set off through the vineyards, Luis explaining everything to her as they progressed along the rows of sturdy vines.

Kate had to admire his vast knowledge of the business and watched with interest the pickers careful expertise as they cut each bunch and placed them in wicker baskets.

'We are careful not to damage the fruit, otherwise fermentation would begin before the fruit reaches the press,' he continued and went on to suggest she may like to look around the vat houses.

Inside the dim vaulted building Kate saw the huge fermentation vats which, once the grapes were crushed, would hold the must. And, in another area, the filters were being prepared and the equipment sterilised ready for use. She met some of the workers who greeted her with a cheery smile and heard the occasional complimentary cry as she passed by.

'It is quite an occasion for them to see such fair beauty at their place of work,' Luis commented as they strolled through to the other end of the building.

It was as they returned to the house for lunch when Luis told her he must leave for Madrid later that afternoon.

'Don't worry, I shall be back the day after tomorrow,' he said, smiling at her look of disappointment. 'It is a business meeting connected with the trade. You will be quite all right here with my family. I know the ladies of the house can be rather tiresome, but I would be most grateful if you can be tolerant. Most likely Marie-Louisa will be in Barcelona for some of the time.'

'Your father is charming,' Kate said truthfully. 'I shall be quite happy chatting to him and, don't worry, I have no intention of upsetting your aunt.'

Luis laughed. 'Good! Then I shall look

forward to my return. Will you miss me?'

'Yes, I'll miss you,' she admitted quietly, inwardly aware she would miss him far more than he realised. And during lunch she found herself preoccupied with her thoughts. She had suddenly discovered she was in love with Luis; there was no other way of accounting for how she felt.

Luis' voice broke into her inner turmoil. 'Perhaps it would be better if you don't go to the vineyard tomorrow,' he advised. 'I have plenty of books you can study.'

'But why?' she asked, unable to conceal her disappointment. 'I'm just getting used to it.'

'I was thinking of Thorpe,' he replied quietly. 'It is just possible he may call.'

'Why should he choose this place? Anyway, he seems more apologetic now so . . .'

'Apologetic? Why do you say that?' Luis broke in sharply. 'Come along, Katherine, exactly what do you mean?'

Flustered, Kate shook her head. 'Nothing really, I just don't think he'll come here.'

'You have good reason for thinking this— haven't you?' Luis pressed, regarding her closely. 'Are you keeping something from me?'

'No—well, not really,' she began then, with a shrug of defeat, confessed, 'He telephoned the hotel Estrella the day before yesterday— in the afternoon.'

'And? Well, Katherine—tell me the rest.'

'He said only that he wished to apologise

for the way he treated me—but really, it was more personal than professional.'

'And you—what did you say?' Luis demanded, his expression grim.

'I simply put down the 'phone,' she replied tightly, annoyed he should cross-question her in front of the others. 'What did you expect I would do?'

'You realise he knew where to contact you,' Luis reminded her. 'He must have heard the announcement at the station.'

'Yes, I'm aware of that, but he doesn't know I am here!' she countered indignantly. 'At the time I didn't know myself.'

'Agreed. However, I prefer you stay indoors,' he directed, his tone imperious as he held her gaze across the table, his dark eyes forbidding her to disagree.

Kate managed to suppress her impulse to argue, purely because the other members of family were seated nearby. But their conversation had aroused his father's curiosity; even appearing to have caught Señora Vendrell's interest when Luis revealed details of John Thorpe's involvement in the wine business. She was furious with herself for letting slip the matter of the telephone call; it seemed she would never be allowed to forget the past.

After Luis left, Kate wondered how well she would fare with the señora during his absence. But, to her relief, his aunt was most

101

pleasant, although she was dismayed to learn that Marie-Louisa was to return from Barcelona the following day. Not that she expected to be bothered by the sometimes spiteful young woman; she intended to study the books Luis had selected.

However, Marie-Louisa returned earlier than expected the next morning, and in a strangely excitable mood. Soon after her arrival she and her mother went off to another part of the house leaving Kate undisturbed until lunchtime.

During lunch the señora and her daughter were utterly charming, which made Kate wonder if she had misjudged them and it was Luis' presence that subdued their apparent preference for today's light and friendly discussion. Only the elder Señor Vendrell remained silent, glancing from one to the other with what seemed to Kate a slightly bewildered expression. She had anticipated mealtimes to be an occasion when she would find the strain of making pleasant conversation exhausting but, surprisingly, the atmosphere between them couldn't have been more relaxed.

'I'd rather like to sit out on the patio today,' she ventured over coffee. 'I want to make the most of this beautiful weather.'

'But Luis was a little concerned about you, my dear,' the señora reminded her, 'as we all are.'

'Katherine can sit with me,' Señor Vendrell invited. 'She will not be alone.'

'Thank you, señor, I will enjoy the company,' Kate smiled. 'And if you wish to sleep I shall not disturb you.'

'Then it is settled,' the señora agreed. 'Marie-Louisa and I have to go out for a while, but as you won't be lonely Katherine we shall not be so anxious about you.'

After they had left, Kate took her books outside and settled into a comfortable lounger whilst Señor Vendrell reclined in another, nearby. She wore a large straw hat to protect her face from the hot sun but stretched her bare legs in front of her in the hope of acquiring a tan. As she stared at the book on her lap, the words mingled, becoming a blur as her thoughts went to Luis. She recalled his smile as he drove away the previous afternoon and experienced a wave of pleasure as she pictured his face.

Lost in her reverie, Kate was startled when a sudden cry came from the direction of the bodega, and from the building ran a young worker who she quickly realised was calling for help.

Rising swiftly to her feet, she remembered there was no-one else in the house and, without waiting to see what the trouble could be, she hurried to meet the young man who appeared extremely distressed.

'Slowly, please,' she said in Spanish after he

blurted out the reason for his alarm faster than she could comprehend. But when he repeated the words more calmly, an icy shiver travelled down her spine.

'Show me where he is,' she urged the young worker and followed him as quickly as she could to the bodega. And when she saw the cause of his distress, cried, 'Get the first aid box, quickly!'

The man lying on the floor was barely conscious when she knelt beside him and saw the blood spurting from a gash in his arm. And, without waiting for assistance, she took the injured limb and applied pressure to reduce the bleeding.

'Go and telephone for a doctor, immediately!' she directed the quaking young man when he brought the first aid equipment. 'And tell him to hurry!'

As he ran off in the direction of the villa, Kate rummaged in the box with one hand, keeping up the steady pressure with the other. She found a sterile pad and bandages which she applied with care, elevating the injured arm against a barrel. A low moan escaped the man's lips as she made him more comfortable, though she avoided moving him more than was necessary in case it should cause further damage. Instinctively, she knew the situation was serious as the injured man's pallor increased and she was relieved to see another worker entering the door.

'Dios!' the man exclaimed and, making the sign of the cross, continued in Spanish, 'Poor Pedro—his mother will have hysterics!'

'Where is his mother?' Kate asked as she noted the injured man's weakening pulse. 'Does she live nearby?'

'Pedro is the son of the cook,' the man informed her and Kate knew the cook, Rosa, already had left for the village and wouldn't return until early evening to prepare dinner.

'We'll see what the doctor says,' Kate decided, 'but perhaps if you speak a few comforting words to our patient, he may understand he is not alone and help is on the way.'

As the newcomer knelt and spoke to his workmate, Kate heard running footsteps and the younger man returned to say the doctor would be here in minutes. 'He lives only two kilometres along the road,' he told her 'and, luckily, he was in when we telephoned.'

Hearing this, Kate sighed with relief; if only Luis had been here, she thought anxiously, his confident authority would have quietened the quickly gathering crowd who speculated loudly as to what the cause of the accident could be.

It had seemed an eternity until the doctor arrived, but in reality it was barely ten minutes before he was running an expert eye and hand over the patient. Señor Vendrell had also appeared on the scene and agreed with the doctor that the man should be moved to the house. With the help of a make-shift stretcher and four strong men from the vineyard, Pedro was transported carefully to a room in the villa wherc he was gently transferred to a bed.

'Who is this young lady?' the doctor asked Señor Vendrell as he inserted the final suture in the wound. 'She did a remarkable job for an amateur.'

She heard Señor Vendrell explain her presence at the villa and, in hesitant Spanish, she added, 'I did almost two years of nurse training before my parents died, so that helped.'

'Your quick action probably saved his life, señorita.' The doctor smiled. 'I hope you will agree to spend a little more time with the patient until I can arrange for him to be moved to hospital.'

'Most certainly, anything to help,' Kate offered. 'What do you want me to look out for?'

The doctor lifted his patient's eyelids in turn as he gave his instructions. 'He's quickly regaining consciousness so I'd like you to sit with him whilst I use the 'phone. Call me if you think it necessary; I shouldn't be too long.'

Kate took up her position on a chair near the bedside as the doctor and Señor Vendrell left the room. The patient, Pedro, opened his eyes for a moment, his dull gaze resting on

Kate before he mumbled something she couldn't catch and moved his arm restlessly on the bed.

'Try to keep still, Pedro,' Kate said softly, adding a comforting, 'I'll be here all the time—you are going to be all right,' and thought she saw a flicker of a smile.

Then, just as she saw him relax, the door burst open and in swept the señora and Marie-Louisa.

'Whatever is happening in this house?' she demanded loudly. 'How dare they put you to so much trouble Katherine—to bring one of the workers into the villa—really!'

Kate put a finger to her lips, afraid the señora would disturb the patient.

'Please,' she pleaded softly, 'he must be kept quiet and I don't mind helping.'

'You are most kind, but the inconvenience!' Marie-Louisa exclaimed in slightly lowered tones. 'Katherine, I can't allow you to do this . . .'

'Will you please leave!' Kate hissed as Pedro's distress increased. 'And send in the doctor.'

'Pah! Luis shall hear of this,' the señora shot back in a threatening tone as they both left, slamming the door behind them.

Their gracious manner had been short-lived, Kate thought crossly and, turning back to her patient, was dismayed to catch the pained expression on his face as he stared up into her eyes.

'Don't worry, I'll look after you,' she soothed, disturbed by his pleading gaze. 'You'll soon be well again.'

'Those women!' the doctor muttered as he came into the room. 'I couldn't help but overhear—you were quite right to ask them to leave.'

Kate gave a short laugh. 'I don't suppose they were too pleased but Pedro was becoming extremely agitated.'

'So would I, in his circumstances. Never mind, the ambulance is on its way and I've arranged for an X-ray to be taken.'

'What about his relatives—do they know what has happened?'

'I asked Señora Vendrell to get a message to his mother.'

'Good, otherwise I would have told her,' Kate volunteered, when she was sure she felt Pedro's hand tighten in hers.

'You are a very thoughtful young lady— Luis has chosen well,' the doctor remarked, and as he checked his patient's pulse, continued, 'I spoke with him only yesterday as he left for Madrid.'

After the ambulance had left, the doctor thanked her once more and drove away, leaving her to gather her composure before she had to face the señora again. Luis had begged her to be tolerant of his aunt but during this recent crisis, for the sake of the patient, it had not been possible.

Brushing the dust from her dress, she braced herself and went into the house prepared to explain and apologise. But, to her astonishment, when she came face to face with the Vendrell women their attitude had changed completely.

'Katherine—you must be exhausted!' the señora exclaimed with some concern, and invited, 'Do sit down and allow me to pour you a drink. Marie-Louisa and I are filled with admiration for what you have done today.'

'Indeed we are,' Marie-Louisa agreed. 'You were wonderful.'

Bewildered, Kate took the chair they indicated when Señora Vendrell placed a glass of brandy in her hand. 'Thank you, but I don't deserve all this praise. I just had to do something—there was no-one else and I couldn't leave the poor man in that state. I'm sorry if I spoke rather sharply . . .'

Before Kate could go any further, the señora raised a hand. 'Please, Katherine, don't apologise. We were at fault for making such a scene.' And shooting Kate a most appealing look, added, 'It is the sight of blood—it upsets me—I did not know what I was saying. I do hope you will forgive me,' she entreated, her hand going to her brow as though she sought to wipe the memory from her mind.

'Please don't worry about it, I quite understand.' Kate smiled, knowing from past experience how differently people react in such circumstances.

'I could never be a nurse,' Marie-Louisa said. 'I'm sure I should faint.'

Kate laughed. 'There was a moment this afternoon when I felt the same,' she admitted, relaxing a little now they had reverted to their more amiable manner. Perhaps the time spent here during Luis' absence would not be so bad after all.

'Katherine,' the señora began a trifle hesitantly, 'I hope you will not be too offended if we go out for a while this evening? My daughter and I must make a visit in the city, but it shouldn't take too long and Señor Vendrell will be in the house.'

'Oh, please do, I'll be fine,' Kate assured her. 'You must not feel you have to stay in on my account.'

'That is kind, and I suggest you rest before dinner. You must be very tired.'

'Yes,' Kate agreed, 'I think I will.'

'Then stay in your room until I call you. Dinner may be a little late and I don't want you to get ready too early.'

'Yes, poor Rosa, she will be upset. I could help her tonight, if you wish.'

The señora brushed the idea aside, saying, 'We will help—you must rest.'

'Then I will wait until you call me. Are you going to visit Pedro?'

'Yes, we are going visiting,' the señora said,

with a tight smile, and to her daughter directed, 'We must hurry, do go and change.'

Kate smiled to herself as they left the room; their change of manner had been so unexpected but she welcomed it, and for the next hour she relaxed, allowing Luis to invade her thoughts as she twirled the glass of brandy in her fingers.

*   *   *

It was as Kate was going to her room that she heard someone moving around in the large kitchen. There was a clattering of metal followed by a sharp exclamation in Spanish and, fearing the worst, she went in to find Rosa on her knees picking up the fallen pans.

'For a moment I wondered what was wrong.' She laughed, going to lend the cook a hand.

'Ah, it is nothing, but it puts me in a worse temper,' Rosa grumbled then, giving Kate a broad smile, complained, 'It is men, as usual, they always keep me waiting, make me late for work!' The plump cook gave a loud sigh of exasperation as she slammed shut the cupboard doors, a frown on her face.

'Have you heard any further news about Pedro?' Kate asked gently. 'I do hope he's improving.'

'Pedro! Where is Pedro? He should have been home hours ago—that is why I am late!'

111

'You mean, you don't know?' Kate asked in shocked surprise. 'Didn't you get the message—Señora Vendrell was to let you know.'

'No, no, I have no word from anyone.' Rosa wailed. 'Tell me, what has happened to my Pedro—please.'

Putting her arm around the cook's shoulder, Kate seated her on the kitchen stool and related what had happened to Pedro that afternoon. 'But now he's in hospital he'll get the best care possible, and Señora Vendrell is visiting him this evening so try not to upset yourself,' she finished, seeing Rosa's anxious expression.

'The señora, she visit Pedro? No, I cannot believe it!' Rosa cried, adding tearfully, 'And she gave me no message.'   .

'Well, if it will help, I will telephone the hospital and enquire how Pedro is,' Kate offered gently. 'Then I can give a hand with dinner.'

'Telephone, yes, but help in the kitchen, no. It is my place to cook, and the work will keep my mind busy.'

Kate went off to make the call and was told that Pedro had regained full consciousness, had a blood transfusion, and was now sleeping naturally. Also, the results of the X-ray were satisfactory. She was delighted to hear the doctor had every hope he would make a quick recovery and went back to tell Rosa the good news.

'I am indebted to you, señorita,' Rosa said, tears of relief streaming down her plump cheeks. She shook Kate's hand warmly, thanking her again before bustling her out of the kitchen.

It eased Kate's mind to know Pedro was not in danger, and now Rosa had bluntly refused her offer of help she made her way to her room. She decided first to take a shower then relax on the bed with a book, but as soon as she had dried herself and put on fresh underwear, she realised how tired she was and slipped between the sheets. It would be almost two hours before dinner was served so she allowed herself to drift into a light sleep.

Kate realised she had slept more soundly than intended when she awoke to a tapping on the door of her room.

'I'm sorry, señora, I didn't intend sleeping so long,' Kate called, rising quickly and slipping on her wrap. Going towards the door, she called, 'Do come in and tell me how you found Pedro . . .'

Her voice trailed away and she took an involuntary step back as the caller entered, closing the door behind him.

'John!' she gasped, 'What are you doing here?'

'I called to see you, Kate,' he said softly, his eyes glinting dangerously as he advanced towards her. 'I wanted to apologise—

remember?'

'Get out of here!' she cried, summoning her courage. 'I shall call the staff.'

'Call them,' he challenged, his lips curling in a sneer as he moved towards her, 'but I don't think anyone will hear at this end of the house.'

'Then I shall call the police,' she retaliated bravely. 'You have no right to be here,' and, drawing her robe around her, she made for the door.

'Not so fast!' he interjected harshly, his bony fingers snaking out to fasten on her wrist. And, yanking her round to face him, said, 'I think the time has come for us to forget our differences—let's kiss and make up.'

'Kiss you? Never!' she cried, struggling to extricate herself from his grip as he dragged her towards him.

With rising panic, and repulsed by his kiss, she managed to pull her head aside, uttering a strangled cry as the light went on and she saw Señora Vendrell and Marie-Louisa framed in the open doorway.

'Yes, you have good cause to look alarmed,' the señora rebuked her harshly. 'How dare you behave this way in my house?'

Immediately Thorpe released her, his expression smug as Kate, almost sobbing with relief at the señora's intrusion, tried desperately to explain.

114

'You're mistaken, Señora Vendrell,' she appealed, pulling the robe back onto her shoulders as she ran towards her, 'he came here uninvited.'

'Come, come, Kate, you asked me here,' Thorpe broke in then, to the señora, explained, 'I'm sorry, señora, I would not have come if I had known.'

'You liar!' Kate cried. 'I asked you to leave!'

'But he is here,' Marie-Louisa put in, her supposed expression of horror quickly replaced by one of curious delight. 'Send them from the house, Mama, immediately!'

'Get out of here, John,' Kate stormed, her anger rising over the situation in which she found herself.

'So, you are acquainted with this man,' the señora observed, her tone almost triumphant. 'Even so, I do not expect you to entertain him here. Such blatant disregard for your hosts is unforgivable!'

'Typically English!' Marie-Louisa sneered. 'I dare not think what Luis will say.'

'I shall tell him myself!' Kate snapped. 'I don't consider I am at fault so I have nothing to fear.' And, casting Thorpe a furious glance, she demanded, 'Get out of my room!'

With a shrug, Thorpe made for the door and, pausing before the señora, said, 'Kate gave me to understand I was free to call whenever I wished—in fact, I ought to warn you, she has done this kind of thing before.'

Trembling and speechless, Kate became fully aware of the implication of his words as he strolled casually from the room. And when the señora thanked him for his advice, her heart sank.

'I suggest you dress and join us for dinner,' the señora said coldly. 'I will allow you ten minutes.'

'But if you will just let me explain . . .'

Señora Vendrell raised her hand in an imperative gesture. 'I prefer not to hear any more about your sordid affair and, if it wasn't for my promise to Luis, I would turn you out of the house!'

'And I wouldn't dream of staying,' Kate retorted angrily, 'but as he's due home tomorrow, I shall speak to him before I leave.'

'Do you think he will listen?' the señora sneered, casting Kate a disdainful look. 'He will be horrified to think my daughter witnessed such a scene!'

'Think what you wish,' Kate responded, her shoulders drooping despondently as she turned away. 'And, thank you, but I prefer not to join you for dinner.'

Once alone, Kate's pent up anger began to subside and, gathering her composure, she took her clothes from the wardrobe. She certainly wasn't going down for dinner but, in case of further confrontations, she was going to get dressed; though the señora was seemingly impervious to her appeal. There

116

was nothing she could do but remain and face Luis, hopeful he would accept her explanation before she left. To leave the villa under a cloud was something she couldn't possibly consider.

She was turning the problem over in her mind when there came a tap on the door. For a second she stiffened, fearing John had returned, but it was Rosa who entered.

'I have brought your dinner,' Rosa said and placed a tray on the bedside table. And, with an expression of concern, she asked, 'Are you not well, señorita?'

'I do have a slight headache,' Kate confessed truthfully, 'and I'm not very hungry.'

'The señora says you do not like my cooking but I do not believe her—you usually eat everything.'

'Oh, that's not true! I love your cooking, Rosa,' Kate assured her. 'I wonder why she said that?'

'Ah, she tries to turn me against you!' Rosa exclaimed, raising her eyes to the ceiling. 'She also did not see my Pedro this evening—another lie!'

Kate sighed. 'Well she certainly gave me the impression it was Pedro she was going to visit, yet, now I think of it, she didn't mention his name.'

'You do not know the señora as I do,' Rosa grumbled, taking off the napkin to reveal a

117

dainty meal, tastefully served. 'I tolerate her only for the sake of Señor Luis and his father,' she added bluntly, placing the tray on Kate's lap.

'Thank you, Rosa, it smells delicious,' she managed with a smile and, as the cook was leaving, remembered to ask, 'Did you see a gentleman come to the house earlier—whilst the señora was out?'

Rosa looked puzzled. 'No, I saw no-one. Were you expecting a visitor?'

'No, I just thought I saw someone in the garden. Thank you, Rosa.'

CHAPTER SIX

Kate hardly slept that night. All she could think of was the dreadful experience of the evening before. Time after time she went through her explanation to Luis when he returned; should she broach the matter immediately, or ask to speak with him privately after he had settled in?

She had just finished resting when Rosa came to say breakfast was awaiting her in the dining room. 'And I shall visit Pedro in hospital this afternoon,' Rosa finished excitedly. 'My neighbour will take me in his car.'

'I'm so pleased for you,' Kate said. 'And do give Pedro my best wishes.'

It helped Kate to know Luis would be returning that day and, determined not to be intimidated by the señora's manner, she went down to breakfast. There was no-one in the dining room but she found a place was laid for her and a steaming coffee pot stood nearby.

The remainder of the day went slowly. Again at lunchtime Kate ate alone; no sign of Luis' father and she began to worry over whether he had heard what had happened the previous day from the señora and was avoiding her. It was as she was dressing for dinner that evening that she heard Luis' car in the drive and, rushing over to the balcony, was in time to see him gazing up in the direction of her window, his rather solemn features breaking into a smile as he caught a glimpse of her above.

'See you at dinner in ten minutes,' he called before disappearing into the house.

With a fast beating heart, Kate added the finishing touches to her make-up and brushed her hair. She was unsure as to whether the pounding of her heart was due to Luis' arrival or the trepidation rising within her, knowing she had a lot of explaining to do. Gathering her composure, she slipped on her sandals and descended the stairs, hearing a murmur of voices coming from the dining room.

Luis glanced up from the sherry he was pouring as Kate entered and his dark eyes held hers, causing her heart to jolt. His was a look of smiling welcome, as though he would have liked to take her in his arms, and the love she felt for him welled up inside making her voice tremble a little as she murmured a greeting.

Throughout dinner Luis held the conversation, speaking of his journey and discussing a new business venture with his father. Marie-Louisa cast him an occasional charming smile and her mother acted the perfect hostess, ensuring those present had everything they desired. Kate listened, her mind sometimes drifting to thoughts of her explanation to Luis when the opportunity presented itself, and gave a start when Luis turned his attention her way.

'You're very quiet, Katherine,' he remarked with a look of concern. 'Are you all right?'

'Amazingly well, considering her activities yesterday,' Marie-Louisa put in with a sly glancc at Kate.

'I said the matter was not to be mentioned again,' the señora rebuked her daughter, 'so please do as I ask.'

'Which matter do you speak of?' Luis queried, his glance travelling from one to the other. 'What has been happening here?'

'Ah, yes, Pedro's accidcnt . . .' his father began, but Kate knew only too well to which matter Maric-Louisa referrcd.

'Luis, I would like a moment with you, in private,' Kate intervened, 'there is something I would like to discuss.'

'Of course,' Luis replied with a puzzled frown, 'though there are a few items I must attend to immediately after coffee. I'm planning a little celebration, but perhaps it would be better to clear up any problems before I do. If you will allow me half an hour, then I will be free.'

Murmuring her thanks, Kate wondered what the celebration Luis spoke of could be; their engagement perhaps? Now she was certain of her love for him, there was nothing she wanted more than to be his wife, but only if he returned that love. Up to now he had ridiculed such an emotion.

Kate decided to take her coffee on to the patio after Luis left for his study. Marie-Louisa had put on some music, rather loud Kate thought, but it faded from her ears as she left the house. Breathing deeply to relax her anxious mind, she stared up at the starlit sky, listening to the country sounds; the faint click of insects and the soft rustle of the trees putting her in a more tranquil frame of mind.

Through the window she could see Luis' father contentedly smoking a cigar, and assumed the señora had gone off to the kitchen to give directions to the staff. The tension throughout dinner was beginning to fade from her thoughts and she put down her cup and saucer and strolled along the path in the direction of the bodega, enjoying the warm night air.

Reaching the twisted shadows of the pitosporum trees she left the path to cut across the lawn, taking in the sweet aroma of the abundant flowering creeper which ran along the outer wall. But suddenly, she hesitated, startled as a tall figure came towards her through the trees.

'Oh, Luis, you frightened me!' she exclaimed with a tremulous little laugh. 'If you are free now, would you like me to come back to the house?'

'No, here will do nicely,' he replied, a cool

edge to his voice as he drew near.

At first his tone surprised her, then she quickly realised the señora may already have spoken to him. 'Before you say any more, there is something I must tell you,' she began, her apprehension rising as a shaft of moonlight filtering through the trees revealed the strange smile on his face.

Wordlessly he stood before her, his dark eyes glittering as he threw down his jacket when, unexpectedly, he took her roughly in his arms and kissed her hard on the mouth.

'It seems you enjoy men who treat you badly,' he hissed, as she drew away from his savage embrace, 'and, as you were willing to allow Thorpe the pleasure of your body, I demand you grant me the same privilege!'

'I did not!' she cried indignantly. 'Please, let me explain . . .'

Her objection was cut short as he captured her mouth once more, lowering her to the grass, his fingers entwined in her hair to prevent her pulling her head aside as he pinned her to the ground.

Suddenly, he raised his head. 'Tell me,' he demanded, 'how do my kisses compare with Thorpe's?'

Shocked and afraid, Kate turned away from his piercing stare. 'Let me go,' she pleaded with a shuddering gasp, 'please, Luis . . .'

'Let you go—after the way you repay my hospitality?' he grated, keeping a firm hold on her trembling body. 'To think that I spent my evenings warning the local vineyards about Thorpe while you were planning to entertain him here!'

'I didn't,' she protested brokenly, 'it's not true!'

'I wish I could believe that!' he snarled, turning her back to face him, compelling her to meet his eyes.

'Please, Luis—you must!' she sobbed desperately, tears coursing freely over her cheeks as she fought against his strength.

Uttering a groan of exasperation, Luis released her, his eyes never leaving her face. 'Madre de Dios!' he exclaimed angrily, 'even I cannot take a woman in tears.' And snatching up his jacket he rose and moved away.

Kate struggled to her feet. 'You beast!' she cried brokenly. 'I'll not stay here a moment longer.'

Hearing this, Luis swung round. 'Oh, no?' he returned fiercely, his stance arrogant. 'Until your uncle returns you are my responsibility.' And with that, he came back and grasped her firmly by the hand.

Objecting wildly at first, Kate held back, but he was determined to get her into the house and, not wishing to humiliate herself further in front of the señora, she tore her hand away and marched ahead of him through the front door, hearing the key turn in the lock as he followed close behind. Without a backward glance she ran up the stairs and went straight to her room where she threw herself on the bed. And, because of the lateness of the hour she had no alternative but to remain there until morning. It was obvious to Kate the señora had wasted no time in giving Luis her account of what had happened during his absence and, now that she loved him, the pain of his contempt was harder to bear.

Kate slept restlessly that night and, during the short time she dozed, her dreams were terrifying, when it was John's lips that sought hers and she couldn't escape. It was only eight o'clock when she heard a knock on her bedroom door and, assuming it was Rosa, she slipped on her dressing gown and went to open it. But it was Luis who entered, his gaze sliding over her as she stood questioningly before him.

'Get dressed,' he commanded, 'you are coming down to breakfast.'

'And if I choose not to . . .?' she retorted with a defiant lift of her chin.

'Then I will assume you can not face my family because of your guilt,' he countered smoothly, 'and your breakfast will be served to you here.'

'I have absolutely no reason to feel guilty,' she retaliated, 'so you can expect me in the dining room in fifteen minutes.'

'Good! I will not start until you join me . . .'

he paused, pointing a warning finger in her direction, 'so do not make plans to leave the house, I shall be watching every door.'

'Go away!' she cried angrily, 'you're the most autocratic beast I've ever met!'

With a mirthless smile Luis left the room, leaving her trembling with indignation. She knew it would take a supreme effort on her part to face his family at breakfast but she was determined not to let her distress show.

It seemed to Kate all eyes were upon her as she entered the dining room. Luis gave her a mocking stare as he pulled back her chair, and Marie-Louisa sniggered into her handkerchief whilst her mother looked on with an air of smiling superiority. Only the elder Señor Vendrell welcomed her in his usual kindly manner, his expression faintly sympathetic.

Kate forced a polite greeting and remarked on the beautiful weather, though inwardly she felt desperately unhappy.

'I do hope my uncle contacts me soon,' she managed brightly. 'I'm so looking forward to seeing him again.'

'Surely you're not thinking of leaving us?' the señora queried, retaining her fixed smile. 'We are just getting to know you.'

'Oh, I wouldn't dream of accepting your hospitality indefinitely,' Kate declined politely. 'In fact, I ought to go into Barcelona today.'

'Have you an appointment?' the señora

asked, equally polite.

'No, but I can wait there until my uncle returns.'

'I think not,' Luis broke in. 'Clive would never forgive me should something happen to you . . .'

Kate bit her lip, determined not to argue in front of the others, though nearly choked on the roll she was eating when he continued, 'and I would like him to hear about your little adventure yesterday.'

'I intend to tell him about that myself,' Kate returned coolly, 'after all, I have nothing to hide.'

'Actually, I was referring to the admirable way you dealt with the accident in the bodega,' he rejoined smoothly with an arrogant lift of his brow. 'We are indeed thankful to you for saving Pedro's life.'

For a moment Kate was speechless. It seemed Luis was doing his best to make her feel uncomfortable. 'Oh, that,' she murmured with a modest shrug, 'I did very little—it was the doctor . . .'

'But I saw what happened, and I was there when the doctor complimented you,' Luis' father put in with a warm smile.

'And Pedro, how is he progressing?' Kate continued. 'Rosa must be very anxious.' And she glanced across to the señora who immediately rose from the table.

'I telephoned earlier and his condition is

good,' Luis told her. 'Naturally, I keep Rosa informed and I have promised to drive her to the hospital today.'

Hearing this, Kate warmed a little towards him. It pleased her to hear he showed concern for his staff; if only he would listen to her side of the story concerning John. Surely he would grant her the right to defend her reputation?

Señora Vendrell had already withdrawn from the room and it wasn't long before the others followed, except Luis and, when Kate made to leave the table, he laid a firmly restraining hand on her arm.

'Where are you going, Katherine?' he asked. 'Remember, you are not to leave the house until I am ready to take you.'

'I am not your prisoner!' she reminded him with increasing anger. 'I shall go where and when I please!'

'Until Clive returns I hold myself responsible for you, and you have some explaining to do before the day is through.'

'I was quite willing to do that last night,' she flung back, 'but now I don't see why I should.'

Rising from his seat he towered above her. 'We shall see!' he ground out through tight lips. 'I only regret I was not here when your lover called.'

'And so do I!' Kate cried indignantly. 'I would also like to know who told him you were away as he wouldn't have risked a confrontation with you. And how did he know

128

where to find me? I know Clive wouldn't divulge my whereabouts so you tell me how he knew? Yes, Luis, someone has a lot of explaining to do,' she ended firmly having gathered a little more composure.

'And who do you suggest?' he enquired with a derisive lift of his brow. 'Do you think my father would encourage such an assignation? After all, my aunt and Marie-Louisa were out at the time.'

'Oh yes, visiting Pedro, or so they would have us believe!' Kate shot back. 'I'm not suggesting your father was at fault, just that he may inadvertently have mentioned you were away and John came into the house without his knowledge.'

'John! Don't you mean Thorpe? Or perhaps you prefer to be on first name terms with a man you profess to dislike?'

'Think what you like, Luis, I'm going upstairs to pack. I won't remain here another minute.'

He gave a harsh laugh. 'And just how far do you think you will get with all your luggage?'

'I would call a taxi,' Kate countered. 'I may not be as helpless as you imagine.' With that she left him standing there, ignoring his hiss of exasperation as she went up to her room.

As Kate took her clothes from the wardrobe, she considered again about how John managed to trace her here, sure that someone else had been involved. She recalled, it didn't surprise him to find her in this room; he'd knocked on the door as though expecting she would answer. Thinking John was a friend of hers, Luis' father may have invited him into the house, but he would never have directed him to her bedroom. That only left the staff, Señora Vendrell, and her daughter, but Rosa hadn't seen anyone and the two women were out at the time. There was no doubt someone wished to defile her reputation and, as Marie-Louisa showed a great interest in Luis, she was the one to gain. She could understand the girl's jealousy yet, surely her mother wouldn't collaborate with her in such a wicked plan—or would she? The señora would see Luis as a good match for her daughter—wealth, a position in society—a mother's aspirations for her offspring? Yet Luis showed little interest in the girl apart from a mildly tolerant attitude towards her rather childish manner.

Strangely, it was as though by thinking about Marie-Louisa she drew the girl to her room, and she was immediately on her guard.

'You are leaving!' Marie-Louisa observed in mock dismay. 'Does Luis know?'

'Yes, I told him this morning,' Kate managed evenly, 'but I don't expect he will be too upset when I'm gone.'

'Quite right, Señorita Shaw,' came a voice from the doorway, 'and the sooner the better for us all.'

'All? Don't you mean the two of you?' Kate

returned, meeting the señora's stony gaze.

'You insolent creature!' the woman hissed. 'You English are all alike.'

'What is it you dislike about the English?' Kate asked. 'Why are you so antagonistic towards us?'

'I have no wish to discuss my reasons with you, señorita. In fact, why Luis bothers to keep you here I will never understand.'

'Nor will I,' Kate agreed, 'and if you will excuse me I would like to finish my packing.' Turning her back on the two women, she folded the last garment into place. Much as she felt inclined to defy the señora, it was impossible for her to remain now Luis had turned against her, however unjust the reason.

Once she had packed, Kate awaited the opportunity to get her cases downstairs and telephone for a taxi, but from the landing she could hear Luis' voice and knew it was hopeless. He would only try to prevent her and she wasn't willing to suffer the indignity of another scene in front of his family.

Almost an hour passed before, from her balcony window, she saw him striding towards the bodega and hurriedly stepped back as he shot a quick glance upwards. At the doorway of the bodega he stopped and spoke to the manager and, to her dismay, he continued to face the house. She knew it was impossible to leave by taxi while Luis was around until it suddenly occurred to her to leave her cases

131

behind and go by way of the rear of the house and walk until she reached the main road. Surely there would be a bus passing, or maybe someone would offer her a lift.

Packing a few small items into her handbag, she checked her money and passport before glancing outside. Luis was standing in the same spot but she was sure he would soon return to the house; she had to leave right away.

Once away from the house she quickened her pace along the dusty track that led to the main road. The sun had risen high into the sky, its rays beating mercilessly upon her as she stumbled over the loose earth.

Almost overcome by the heat, she stopped beneath the shade of a tree. There were two cottages ahead of her and, in the distance, she spotted the sun's glittering reflection from the cars travelling along the main road. A woman emerged from one of the small white houses and, as she drew near, Kate recognised the heavy build of the dark-haired cook.

Rosa immediately threw up her hands in horror and cried, 'What are you doing walking on this road in the hot sun—you will burn your beautiful skin, señorita.'

'I'm all right, Rosa,' Kate hurriedly assured her, taking a nervous glance over her shoulder. 'I'm going back to Barcelona, but I prefer you don't mention you have seen me.'

'Why not?' Rosa asked, wide-eyed with

curiosity. 'You are running away?'

'Of course not,' said Kate, a little crossly. 'I just thought it would be a change to walk and hail a taxi on the main road.'

'A walk—in this heat?' Rosa spread her hands in an expressive gesture. 'Señorita, I don't believe you, I think the señora has sent you away, yes?'

'Well, in a way, yes,' Kate admitted. 'She was certainly delighted to know I was leaving, but Luis . . .'

'Ah, Señor Luis, he would never send you away,' Rosa beamed. 'He is enamoured of you.'

'Not any more, I'm afraid,' Kate admitted, feeling her lower lip tremble.

Rosa dismissed Kate's words with a sweep of her plump hand. 'He has such pride, but here,' she laid a hand on her breast, 'in his heart he is a very good man.'

'I'm not so sure, he's quite an arrogant beast when he chooses!'

'What do you want,' Rosa demanded, 'a weak-minded boy or a real man?'

'Look, Rosa, I value your advice, but I really must press on, and I'll be grateful if you don't mention seeing me to anyone.'

'To the señora and her stupid daughter, no I will not tell. But to Señor Luis and his father I am loyal so, if the señor asks, I shall tell him,' Rosa declared, adding knowingly, 'I suspect the señora is behind this and you should not allow her to hurt you—you English, you don't understand.'

'What is this about the English?' Kate demanded. 'The señora appears to have a great dislike of us—her daughter too.'

'Are you blind? Can you not see that the señora wishes her daughter betrothed to Señor Luis,' Rosa cried dramatically. 'She herself failed to become mistress of the villa when his father married an English woman, so now she is determined the position shall be filled by her daughter. You are the second to be banished from the villa—ah, I say too much!'

Rosa's angry explosion left Kate speechless. Her curiosity regarding Luis' mother had been aroused, but the cook would say no more. She compressed her lips and, stuffing her apron into the worn basket she carried, turned away up the dusty track.

'Well, I'll not change my mind now,' Kate muttered, more to herself now Rosa had put some distance between them.

Once she turned on to the main road, Kate watched for the sign of a bus stop at the roadside. Already she felt weary and her mouth was dry; the thought of a long walk before a bus came daunted her determination. She became aware of the curious stares from the drivers of passing cars and began to feel a trifle nervous. Perhaps it would be more sensible to refuse a lift should she be offered one, yet there was no bus stop in sight and she realised her pace was getting slower and the heat becoming more unbearable as she progressed. And when she heard the screech of brakes behind her, tired though she was, she prepared to refuse the offer of a lift and didn't turn at the blast of a horn.

'Where the devil do you think you're going?' came a voice she instantly recognised, and she turned to see Luis slam the door of his car and come striding towards her.

'It's no use shouting. I'm not coming back with you,' she told him firmly.

'Get in the car, at once!' he directed. 'You will collapse in this heat.'

'No, no, I won't,' she protested weakly as Luis reached her side. But she had no more strength to object as the ground reeled about her.

'You little fool!' she heard him mutter and felt herself being swept up in his arms as the strange weakness enveloped her completely.

Gradually, Kate became aware that the cool air on her face came from the folded newspaper Luis was fanning in front of her. She was in the passenger seat of his car which he had set in a reclining position and, as her vision cleared, she saw his look of deep concern fade, to be replaced by a sardonic smile.

'So, my little butterfly tried her wings and failed, yes?' he said softly.

135

'You don't have to remind me,' she told him in a wavering voice. 'And, thank you, I'll be all right now.'

'Surely you do not intend to continue on foot,' he exclaimed scornfully. 'You wouldn't get very far in this heat.'

'Well, I'm not going back with you, whatever you say, and while I'm in your car I don't trust you not to try and force me.'

'Even if I plead with you, Katherine?'

'No, Luis, please don't make me. I realise Rosa thought she was doing the right thing when she told you where to find me . . .'

'Rosa? What has she got to do with it—I haven't seen her since breakfast.'

'I met her back along the road,' Kate sighed. 'I thought she'd told you.'

'No. I wasn't aware you had left until I went to your room to tell you Clive was on the telephone.'

'Oh, I see. What did he say?'

'He was as surprised as I that you had left the house, though you can relax as I didn't mention why.'

'As I told you once before, I have nothing to hide. Now, what else did he have to say, is he coming back to Barcelona?'

'Yes, this evening, and now I realise it is hopeless trying to persuade you to come back with me, I will drive you into Barcelona.'

'You will drive me?' she queried warily. 'I can just as easily take a bus.'

136

'Do not be so ridiculous!' he growled as he turned on the ignition. 'I already have your cases in the boot so I may as well take you as well. I notice you did not get very far with them yourself.'

'I didn't even try,' she replied wearily, repressing a desire to let him have a piece of her mind. 'My only thought was to get away from the villa.'

'Then why bother to haul them downstairs?'

'Downstairs?' she echoed disbelievingly. 'I left them in my room.'

'Why must you argue? They were standing in the hall when I answered the telephone.'

'Why must I argue?' She let out a long sigh. 'Oh, Luis, you are insufferable!'

To her surprise, Luis made no comment but let in the clutch and pulled away, quickly gathering speed as he looked straight ahead, his mouth set in a grim line.

'I'll bring in your luggage,' he said coolly when they reached the hotel. 'And, one last word of advice—watch what you do until Clive arrives. I would like to have met him again but, in the circumstances, maybe it is better I don't. Instead, I will visit Pedro and then I must get back to work.'

Kate couldn't bring herself to reply and merely murmured her thanks as she walked ahead of him into the hotel. And only after he had ensured there was a vacant room did she steal a last glance at his retreating figure as he walked swiftly away from the desk to disappear into the busy street.

CHAPTER SEVEN

Clive reached the hotel about seven o'clock that evening when the inevitable questions Kate had dreaded were asked.

'I'll go into that later,' Kate replied when he asked why she was back at the hotel sooner than expected, 'but first, I want to hear about your travels and how you fared.'

'Well, to begin with, we have Luis to thank for the good business I've done in Rioja. He soon reported our unscrupulous acquaintance, Thorpe, to the Ministry of Agriculture in Madrid who in turn warned the officials of each region. By now almost every vineyard will be aware that Thorpe may try to trade with them so that should put an end to his illegal racket for good, particularly in this area, which is why I've left the Penedes region until the last. As soon as Thorpe finds no-one will have dealings with him, he will leave the country and I don't think he'll dare try it again.'

'Thank goodness for that,' Kate said with relief yet, considering it was only two days since John had appeared at the villa, she doubted he would be out of the country.

'And how have you spent your time?' Clive asked suddenly, making Kate start. 'Is Luis joining us for dinner tonight?'

'I-I don't think so,' she stammered uncomfortably. 'He's rather busy.'

'I would have thought you'd have stayed longer than this. Surely they haven't finished picking already?'

It took a moment for Kate to calm herself and, taking a gulp of her wine, she eventually managed to relate all that had happened during his absence. But not quite all; she left out the incident in the garden when Luis had vented his angry passion upon her after he had learned of Thorpe's visit.

'The very cheek of the devil!' Clive exclaimed angrily. 'I must have a word with Luis about this . . .'

'No, I'd rather you didn't.' Kate broke in. 'If Luis can't take my word then he's not worth bothering about.'

'Just as you wish, Kate,' he conceded, 'but I expect he was jealous. The people of the Catalan region have a great deal of pride and it was bound to upset the family.'

'The family!' Kate cried indignantly. 'I was the one most upset by it all, but that doesn't seem to matter.'

'Of course it does, my dear,' Clive smiled, laying a comforting hand on Kate's. 'Tell you what, we'll go to the wine festival in Sitges tomorrow, that will help to cheer you up.'

'Oh, I really don't feel like going anywhere,' Kate declined. 'Actually, I was wondering when we were going home.'

140

'Going home—nonsense! I still have some business to attend to and I can conduct it in Sitges during the festival.'

The following day Kate and her uncle set off in a hired car which took them southwards along a winding coastal road to the small town of Sitges. There they mingled with the crowds in the narrow streets to watch the parade of ponies in polished festival harness pulling carts laden with grapes. And at the end of the promenade, at the foot of the steps leading to the church, they applauded the local dignitaries seated on a platform when the Queen of the Harvest was named and duly crowned.

After this ceremony was completed, Clive suggested lunch which they took in an hotel overlooking the sea. 'Thought you might like to get out of the sun,' Clive said with a whimsical smile, 'though already I notice you've acquired a slight tan.'

'What will you do after lunch?' she asked him.

'I'm going to visit an old acquaintance of mine who lives not far out of town. His vineyard produces excellent wines and I'm sure you will enjoy meeting him.'

It was almost four when they left the hotel and went on to the vineyard Clive had spoken of. His old business associate turned out to be a charming man who welcomed them both with typical courtesy.

Kate joined in with their wine tasting but discovered it extremely difficult to decide which wine belonged to which grape or year. Even so, she found it interesting just to watch the two men enjoying each other's company as they gave their professional appraisal to the wines.

Suddenly, she realised her uncle was speaking. 'Are you tired, Kate?' he asked, adding a trifle disappointedly, 'I thought you would have enjoyed a little tasting, but if you'd rather go . . .'

'No, of course not. I'm sorry, I was miles away. It's all fascinating,' she ended convincingly, looking around her to the huge barrels and the strange assortment of implements used by the wine maker.

'The young señorita should join the celebrations in Sitges tonight,' the proprietor suggested heartily. 'It is a time of rejoicing for the vineyard workers, the growers, and all lovers of good wine!'

Clive shot her an enquiring look. 'Maybe Kate is a little tired . . .'

'Nonsense, she is young!' the older man disagreed. 'When we have concluded our business, the three of us will go and join the festivities.'

Much as she would have preferred to be left alone, Kate hadn't the heart to disappoint them and half an hour later they were driving back to Sitges. Darkness had fallen by the time they reached the promenade and the scene which met her eyes caused her to gasp with delight.

The church, flanked by tall palms was now illuminated, the profile of its mellow peach walls clear and beautiful against the night sky, its foundations bathed by the sea. And, beneath the church, on the coloured paving of the promenade, people danced to a small band; a reedy-sounding group of instruments like she had never heard before.

'The church looks magnificent in this setting!' she exclaimed delightedly. 'And the dance—it's a strange step—I don't think I could ever master it.'

'Come, I will show you,' the older man offered. 'Soon the music will begin again and it starts more slowly so you can learn.' And he took her hand as a few bars were played on a whistle followed by a number of quick beats on a tiny wrist drum.

She was giving her full attention to the steps and was hardly aware of the hold on her left hand being released until it was taken in a firmer warm grip and she heard a voice say, 'Perdon, señor!' Glancing sideways she found it was Luis who had taken her hand and her heart seemed to stand still when she lost the rhythm of the dance completely.

'Katherine, I must speak with you,' Luis said, drawing her aside as the circle closed once more.

143

'But Clive—he will wonder where I am,' she protested.

'I have already spoken to Clive; he knows you are with me,' he assured her. 'I have been searching for you most of the day until it suddenly occurred to me you may be here in Sitges for the festival.'

'You have been searching for me?' she said in disbelief. 'But why, Luis, what do you want?'

'I thought you should know that Thorpe has left the country.'

'You could have told me that over the telephone, so why search for me here?'

He hesitated in his step and taking both her hands said gently, 'Because I did not want to lose you, Katherine.'

'But you were very eager to move my belongings out of your house,' she countered, 'and quite willing to drive me back to the hotel. In fact, you didn't even say goodbye.'

'I needed time to consider why I had treated you so badly,' he sighed and, looking searchingly into her eyes, appealed, 'Can you ever forgive me?'

Kate turned her head away, finding it difficult to make a suitable reply. 'I don't know what to say . . .' she managed at last, 'you don't trust me, Luis.'

'Ah, but since you left I have learned the truth about what happened at the villa.'

'Why couldn't you simply have taken my

144

word for it?' she objected, walking ahead. 'You never gave me the opportunity to explain.'

He shrugged expressively. 'I will admit I was unreasonably jealous—a family failing, I'm afraid—something I inherited from my father.'

'In connection with your mother?' Kate put in and knew by his sudden silence she had touched upon a delicate subject. 'Tell me about her, Luis,' she coaxed gently, pausing by the iron railings to stare out to sea.

'I suppose you are bound to be curious,' he granted, coming to a halt beside her, 'and I have only just learned from Rosa exactly what happened all those years ago. I believe my father eventually suspected something was amiss.'

'Rosa told me your aunt drove your mother away. Is that true?'

'Yes, she contrived to degrade her in my father's eyes, but he realises that now.'

'That was a wicked, thing to do, but what happened to your mother after that?'

'Unable to bear the recriminations, my mother left. Sadly, she was killed in a car accident as she drove from the villa and my father has never forgiven himself.'

'How very sad,' Kate sighed. 'But he shouldn't blame himself . . .'

'That was five years ago and, at the time, I suppose I also blamed her for my father's distress, but now . . .' He broke off and brought down his fist, striking the railing in a fierce gesture, adding remorsefully, 'But now I know the truth!'

'But why has Rosa waited all these years to tell you?' Kate asked. 'It could have saved a lot of unhappiness if she had spoken up before.'

'Ah, but Rosa was a widow with a large family to support and my aunt threatened to dismiss her if she revealed anything to my father.' Luis shook his head, adding sadly, 'Poor Rosa, she is filled with remorse.'

'But you will forgive her, Luis? She was in a difficult position.'

'Of course,' he agreed, 'particularly as she couldn't stand by and allow it to happen again. Pedro spoke of this only yesterday after his mother told him of the conversation she had overheard between Marie-Louisa and my aunt. Evidently Marie-Louisa contacted Thorpe through the hotel Estrella as it seems he had heard the announcement at the station when you first arrived and had bribed the young telephonist to let him know of your movements. I also discovered the telephonist knew where to contact Thorpe and for a further sum of money he had given this information to my cousin.'

'Oh, it's all so horrible,' Kate shuddered. 'Yet I can't see how they knew the hotel would have the information.'

146

'I wasn't sure at first, then I remembered one evening at dinner, when you admitted Thorpe had phoned you at the hotel and I noticed how my aunt took an unusual interest in the conversation. I suspect it was then the idea came to her as she couldn't help but notice how furious I was at the time.'

Kate sighed and looked him straight in the eyes. 'But it has taken all this for you to believe in my innocence, Luis.'

'Of course not!' he exclaimed passionately. 'I had realised my true feelings for you well before this happened. My aunt is very persuasive though and easily aroused jealousy in me.'

'Then I suppose we should feel sorry for her—a loveless woman . . .'

'Sorry!' he exploded. 'My dear Katherine, because of her you would have left. I nearly lost you . . .' He reached out, and drawing her into his arms, pleaded, 'Please tell me I have not lost you.'

Kate allowed herself the comfort of his arms and rested her head against his broad chest, feeling the strong beat of his heart. 'No, Luis, you haven't lost me,' she admitted a trifle breathlessly.

Lifting her face to his, he whispered hoarsely, 'Katherine, I love you,' then kissed her gently on the mouth.

As their lips drew apart she gave a nervous little laugh. 'But I didn't think you believed in

147

love,' she reminded him. 'You once called it a stupid emotion.'

He uttered a long sigh. 'Yes, I was very bitter,' he confessed, 'and I suppose I wanted to hurt you because of what my mother had done, or what I thought she had done, but then I fell in love with you and had to struggle with my emotions. Regardless of what happened at the villa, I knew I wanted you to be my wife and I wish to welcome you back to my home.'

'B-but, I couldn't,' Kate stammered, 'not with your aunt there, I just couldn't.'

'Do not worry about that. I demanded she leave the house, and my father also threatened to cut off the generous allowance he granted her if she didn't move out immediately. Needless to say, money is her greatest love so she and her wicked daughter have already left for Madrid.'

'Oh, I see,' Kate said with relief. 'But what about Clive? I can't let him down.'

'That is no problem. Clive has already agreed to take a partner who is well acquainted with the wine trade—a fair exchange, don't you think?'

'You've got it all worked out,' she accused him laughingly.

'I had to work quickly, Katherine, because I want you to be my wife. Not for the reason I originally intended,' he added quickly, 'but because I love you very deeply.'

148

'Oh, Luis,' was all Kate could murmur before he kissed her once more.

'Come, querida,' he whispered as their lips slowly drew apart. 'Tonight we have more to celebrate than the wine festival. Let us join in the dancing before I take you back to the villa.'

From somewhere in the distance, floating on the soft evening air, came the sound of a passing train, a train to Barcelona, perhaps. Kate smiled to herself, snuggling closer into the circle of Luis' arm as they strolled back along the promenade.